Counselor Stories

Barbara Brunk Sharkey

ISBN 978-1-304-50177-6

To my family,
both present now
and those who have gone before

Chapter One: Roberta

May, 2011

By the time the fourth person had arrived in the small waiting room, it was obvious that something was seriously amiss.

"But she's never late. I just don't understand." Roberta Lovell snapped her cell phone closed after dialing her therapist's number for the fifth time since she'd arrived for her noon appointment.

"She's been late for me," the large, balding man in the chair against the far wall said. "Lots of times."

"That's only if it's a one o'clock," the woman in sweatpants and an old sweatshirt on the couch murmured, the first words she'd spoken since Roberta had entered the room nearly an hour ago. "And she always adds on the time at the end. But she never, ever, just doesn't show."

The three speakers looked expectantly at the newest arrival, a skinny girl who had taken the last seat available when she arrived moments earlier, a straight-backed wooden chair squeezed between the couch and the door. She perched nervously on the edge of the chair, her large waifish eyes making her look very much like a deer about to bolt at the least provocation. She shook her head slightly to indicate she had nothing to add to the conversation.

When the door opened again it was Dr. Fleming, who, beyond startled, was clearly aghast at the full room.

"What are you all doing here?" he asked in surprise.

"Waiting for Liz, of course," Roberta answered. "We're getting worried."

"Didn't you see the note? Wasn't there a note on the door?" He stuck his head out and looked wildly around the hallway. "I asked the receptionist next door in mortgage to put up a note." He observed the group sadly and leaned against the wall.

Roberta felt as if she were having an out-of-body experience as she watched Liz's partner take a deep breath in an effort to calm himself. Something was terribly wrong, she was sure of it.

"I'm sorry to have to tell you this. I received a message that Liz was in a car accident this morning. She's in intensive care. I'm headed to the hospital now."

"I knew she'd never be late," Roberta said, mostly to herself. "How bad is it?"

"What happened? What should we do?" The woman in sweats burst into tears.

"But…but…she just can't be hurt!" The skinny girl finally came to life.

The three women were all talking at once, and the combination of their intense anxiety on top of his own stress nearly sent Dr. Fleming, expert advisor of others, reeling from the scene.

"Look, all of you, go back home," he managed to compose his thoughts. "Call the office and get my voice mail. Leave me your name and number, and I'll get back to you. I can cover your sessions for a while. But not this week. Now I'm going to the hospital to see what I can find out."

With that he left as abruptly as he had arrived, completely forgetting what he had come to the office to get—Liz's appointment book.

The group sat in stunned silence.

"We should send some flowers or something," Roberta finally said.

"That's a good idea," the woman in sweats agreed softly.

"I'll do it," Roberta offered. "Give me your names and phone numbers and I'll let you know what it costs. You can send me a check."

"I'm paperless now," the man said, standing up slowly and reaching for his wallet. "How 'bout if I give you a twenty?"

"That's fine."

"Here's my number," the other woman said, holding out a card.

"Thank you—" Roberta glanced down, "Donna. I'll let you know." She looked at the business card again. "You're Donna Noyes of the Noyes Garden Center fame?"

"Yes. Though not for long. It's my husband's family, and we're about to divorce." Donna's voice trembled on the word "divorce."

"Oh, I'm sorry."

"Here's a twenty from me, too." The skinny girl held out a crumpled bill.

"Well, that's that, I guess. I'll see what I can do."

Roberta was the first to leave, a deep sense of dread overwhelming her as she got into her car. The weekly noontime session with Liz had become her small lifeline, and now the whole hour had been spent sitting and waiting in the office, becoming more agitated as the minutes ticked by. Roberta didn't feel her life was so terrible, it was simply out of whack. Slightly skewed in an uncomfortable direction. In one month her first set of twin daughters would graduate from college, and both were floundering like new ducklings in the water for the first time, trying to set a course for the rest of their lives. And even though Roberta knew that in the end everything would be all right, it was still painful to watch. The second set of twin girls were about to graduate from high school. The thought of getting the two of them through the next month of prom, graduation and then ready to fledge from home in the fall was too much to think about. She had gone back to work three years ago to help with college costs, but her part-time job as the assistant office manager of a large medical group did not really fulfill her. Although she had at first enjoyed the people she worked with immensely, now it was as if the cares and burdens they brought to work simply added to her own mountain of despair. And now this. Shit.

The drive-through line at her usual post-session Seattle coffee shop was too long, so she parked and went in. Coffee in hand, she realized the man from Liz's office was sitting in the corner, his back against the wall, sipping his drink while he observed her. It seemed odd that he had beaten her to the shop. Perhaps she was having memory loss and senior moments on top of everything else. He nodded in recognition as her gaze fell on him, and she walked around some tables so that she could exit past him.

"This your first stop, too?" she asked.

"Recovering alcoholic. I always need a strong shot of something after baring my soul to Liz for an hour."

"I need the caffeine to get through the rest of the afternoon," Roberta smiled wearily. "Thanks for the money. I'll get to work on the flowers." She hesitated, unsure whether to head on out the door or stay. He pushed the chair opposite him out a bit with his foot. She glanced at her watch, saw she still had twenty minutes before she was due back, and sat down.

"My name's Roberta," she took another sip of the soothing, double-tall latte.

"I'm Tony." He swirled his unsweetened, drip coffee in the cup, then leaned in and lowered his voice. "I think her ex-husband tried to kill her."

Roberta choked on the sip she had been swallowing. "What?"

"I bet it was her ex-husband. Lousy guy."

"How do you know that? I don't know anything about her personal life."

"We go way back. Ten years."

"Ten years?" Roberta's eyebrows shot up like arrows. "What the hell is wrong with you? You're not a sex offender or something awful, are you?" Visions of possible addictions beyond alcohol and coffee began swirling in her head.

"No, no, nothing like that." He paused, seeming to size her up, then relaxed back in his chair. "I grew up back East. Everyone there has a therapist. For life. Really."

He said it in separate sentences, as if sparing her the trouble of doubting him.

Roberta had a strong urge to remove herself from both the conversation and his presence, and scooted her chair back a bit so she could make a polite exit.

"Wait, don't go. I'm serious about this," Tony pleaded quietly. "She actually had quite a difficult life, despite the calmness she exuded in sessions."

"You really think her ex-husband could have harmed her?"

"There are other possibilities."

"Like what?"

"Like a jealous wife. Or a wacko client."

Roberta's radar, which had always been good but had become even more precisely tuned in the three years of working with the public in the medical office, was going off at full tilt. She spoke very slowly. "Is she having an affair with a married man?"

"I don't think so," now Tony's voice was nearly flippant. "I just threw that one in."

Roberta was beginning to understand how wacko clients could easily come into play, and she was anxious to put some distance between herself and the one sitting across from her.

"I see I'm scaring you off," Tony said apologetically. "You don't know me and I'm telling you all this weird stuff. I always see the worst in every situation. But I'm harmless, I promise." Reaching into his back pocket, he pulled out his wallet. "Look, here's my card. If you run into anything with bad vibes about Liz, give me a call, maybe I can help."

The neatly printed card merely said, "Tony Wagner" with a phone number beneath. That was it. She turned the card over: blank. She looked at Tony and smiled her office manager smile. Vibes? The only vibe she was feeling was to get out—now.

Back at her office, Roberta called the nearby florist to order the flowers, but was surprised to learn privacy laws had made deliveries much more difficult, and they had simply cut out the service. Undeterred, she decided to swing by after work, pick up the flowers, and transport them to the hospital information desk herself.

Her attempt was unsuccessful, and six hours later she was back home, confused and uncertain. Her husband and the girls had eaten leftovers and gone their separate ways. Roberta set her lovely vase of flowers on the kitchen counter and then scoured the three TV news stations' online sites for information about car crashes in the morning. She found nothing. The receptionist at the hospital desk had refused to take the flowers, simply saying she would not be able to deliver them. Fibbing a bit that the flowers were from co-workers, Roberta finally got out of the person that Liz was not in the hospital. Could Dr. Fleming have had the wrong information, or perhaps Liz had already been released?

The next day Roberta decided to stop at the counseling office at the end of her lunch, hoping to catch Dr. Fleming between clients since none of her phone calls to him had been returned. Opening the hall door quietly she was surprised to discover the skinny girl from the day before sitting on the couch eating a good-looking sandwich.

"What are you doing here?" Roberta asked. "Is Liz back?"

"Uh, no." The girl swallowed her mouthful before trying to continue. Roberta recognized the guilty look that was spreading across her face from many inquisitions with her own girls.

"Look," the girl started apologetically, "my parents are making me come here. My mother drives me over, she waits in the car. She gives me the money for Liz. I just thought, hey, she'll be back in a few days, I'm sure. I'll sit here and absorb the calmness of the atmosphere. That's therapeutic in itself."

"And pocket the hundred and thirty from your parents that you're supposed to be giving her."

"Something like that."

"How old are you?"

"Twenty-two."

Geez, Roberta thought. The same age as the older twins, but this girl seemed much younger by comparison.

"You won't say anything, will you?"

"No, your secret is safe with me. And Liz probably *will* be back soon. She wasn't in the hospital after all. I want to catch Dr. Fleming between sessions and ask about her. He hasn't returned my calls. And there wasn't anything on the news last night about any bad car accidents around here."

"Dr. Fleming's not here. He's got a sub coming in…that elderly woman who covers for them sometimes."

Roberta once again felt there was an entire world going on in this office that she knew nothing about.

"How often are you here?" she asked as the girl finished her last bite.

"Three times a week. My parents think I'm crazy and that I have an eating disorder. Liz is trying to help me break free from their clutches and launch myself into the big world. I hope she gets back soon. We were about to have a big showdown with them."

No wonder you're hanging onto your parents' money. It's breakout time.

"Have you ever picked up any personal information about Liz in your sessions? Where she might live, is she married, any of that?"

"She had a rotten first marriage…married the wrong guy too young, but had kids so she stayed with him too long. I don't think she's in a relationship now; she never talks about it. The kids are grown and live out of state."

That fit with the way Liz was so sympathetic to the burgeoning empty nest Roberta would face in the fall.

"I wonder who's taking care of her dog if she's laid up somewhere?" the girl asked.

"She has a dog?"

"Yep, she brought him a few times for me to see. Dog therapy, she said."

"Listen, um—what's your name? I'm Roberta, like I said yesterday."

"I'm Chrissy."

"Ok, Chrissy. Remember the man who was here yesterday? He's convinced something bad has happened to Liz. And when I went to deliver the flowers, she wasn't at the hospital. Now Dr. Fleming is missing, too. I don't quite know what to do."

"Why don't you call the others? Maybe they'll have an idea. Here's my cell. I don't know if I can be of any help, but my boyfriend works security. My parents don't know about him, though, so, you know, depending on when you call me, I might not be able to talk. He's a little bit older," she added, when the corners of Roberta's mouth did that motherly thing, "but he's really smart."

Roberta sighed. Chrissy was making her more and more depressed. How many interesting secrets did her own daughters have?

Returning to work, Roberta thought more about her girls. One child at a major milestone in life would have been plenty. To have four teetering on the brink made her feel like leaping from a tall building. People were always telling her how easy it must be to have girls after girls. Well, not particularly. From what she could see of her friends with sons, raising boys required only two things: plenty of food in the house and multiple pairs of jeans.

Roberta spent a good part of the afternoon at work checking her cell phone to see if there were any messages from Dr. Fleming. There weren't.

That evening after dinner, Roberta closeted herself in the den and got out Donna Noyes' card. After several rings Donna came on the line, but her voice was muffled, as if she had been crying.

"Donna? It's Roberta, Roberta Lovell, from Liz's office yesterday?"

"Oh, yes."

"I'm sorry, have I caught you at a bad time?"

"It's all a bad time right now. Could you get the flowers?"

"Yes, but something very odd is going on. Liz wasn't in the hospital after all, and I haven't been able to get a hold of Dr. Fleming, either. He has a sub coming in to the office who was no help at all with any information, and he isn't returning phone calls. I don't know what to think."

"The Fleming family goes to my church. I don't know them well, but that's how I heard about the counseling office and started seeing Liz. I know someone who is his wife's good friend. I'll see what I can find out and call you right back."

"Okay, thanks."

It took half an hour before the phone rang for Roberta. In between there had been three 800 sales calls and two calls for her daughters, which she requested be redirected to their cell phones. Finally, Donna called, her voice sounding much better.

"It does seem a little strange," she began, "but apparently the whole family left in a hurry last night for Michigan. Some kind of family emergency. That's about all anyone knows."

"Dr. Fleming, too?"

"I think so."

"Well, that's coincidental, I'd say. I don't know what to do, now."

"Have you thought about driving past her house, just to see how things look?"

"I don't know where she lives, do you?"

"I'm pretty sure it's on one of the streets just above Carkeek Park. About two months ago, at one of my first sessions, she told me that her garden had been featured in the Sunday paper in the magazine section. She knew I worked at the nursery and it was an easy ice breaker to talk about flowers. She was very insistent about privacy and they used a false name and nothing about the location, but when I went home and looked at it, I recognized the view in one of the pictures. There are only about four streets in the city that have that particular view, and they're all above the park."

"You think I should go drive around until I find her house? What then?"

"Maybe you'd find some clues, you know, maybe she's back home and everything is fine. Or maybe the newspapers are all piled up."

"That skinny girl from yesterday? Her name's Chrissy. She said Liz has a dog, and she wondered who was taking care of it. So maybe I could find the dog."

"It's worth a try. We've got to find her. It's only been two days and I'm going crazy without her. The title of the article was something about 'Winter into Spring in the Garden.' I'd try the first couple Sundays in March."

"Thanks. I'm sorry you're feeling off. Things going badly with the divorce?"

"In the toilet. We were married for twenty-five years, have three children, and my husband fell in love with one of the cashiers at the store. Now, despite the fact that I've worked at that nursery since before we got married, he thinks because it's his family's business no part of it should come to me. My daughters aren't speaking to him, my son isn't speaking to me. And I can barely crawl out of bed each day because working at that nursery is all I know how to do."

"Oh, I know that stuck-in-bed feeling. How long has it been?"

"He walked out six months ago."

"That's tough. And Liz's been a help, though, right?"

"The fact that I haven't murdered my husband is proof of that. He's the one who should be sending her flowers."

"Okay. Well, thanks for the tip about the house. I'll see what I can find. The Dents can probably help me look it up online in the paper's archives...maybe I won't have to wait till tomorrow to go to the library."

"I'm sorry, what's your child's name?"

"Oh, *the Dents.* It's family shorthand for our younger daughters. We have two sets of twin girls, four years apart. The first two are fraternal, and we always just referred to them as 'the Twins' even though it's breaking every rule in twindom. Then four years later the second set came along, but they were identical. We somehow fell into calling them 'the Dents.' It's an affectionate term, really."

"And how old are all these girls?"

"The twins are about to graduate from college, the Dents from high school."

"Oh my God, no wonder you're in counseling. Double prom dresses, double hormone-laden dates, and double the after-prom spend-all-night-out-going-who-knows-where plans to argue over. And all leading up to double the "last-time-to-see-my-friends forever" angst all summer long! I can't imagine. My oldest daughter is only 17, but I've heard stories."

"It does feel a little overwhelming at the moment, it's true. I was desperately looking forward to a peaceful hour with Liz yesterday. She seems to put it all into perspective so well."

"Right. She's sympathetic but inspires you to keep up the good fight. You gotta find her. Fast."

"Thanks for your help. I'll call you if I come up with anything."

Roberta managed to peel Dent One away from her cell phone long enough to get help getting into the paper's archives, and, sure enough, a three-page layout of a lovely garden with a view of Puget Sound graced the cover of the magazine on the first Sunday in March. Roberta printed the pictures and then called Chrissy, who agreed to come help look for the house and the dog. She would pick her up in front of the mall at one o'clock the next day.

That night Roberta tossed and turned so much in bed that her husband finally asked what was wrong. Hal was a wonderful man whom she loved deeply, but the upcoming changes with the girls were not affecting him in the same way. He seemed to imagine some magical freedom coming with the Dents' departure (and their boyfriends' departures, their girlfriends' departures, as well as the boyfriends' of the girlfriends departures,) whereas she could only imagine, despite all her current complaining about the chaos, how quiet her life was going to be.

On the third street Roberta and Chrissy cruised, they found the house. A slow pass revealed a black and white Labrador mix racing back and forth across the front fence, and Chrissy immediately identified it as the right dog. Roberta parked the car and they walked up to the front gate.

"Hello, Poochie. Remember me?" Chrissy opened the latch.

"Wait, we can't just go in," Roberta said cautiously.

"Why not?" Chrissy was already inside on her knees, the dog creeping up to her on its belly and then switching to its back for a stomach rub. "He's the sweetest dog, and look, he's starving for attention."

Roberta was still standing uncertainly outside the gate. With Poochie at her heels, Chrissy walked up to the porch.

“Look, the papers are all up here, and the mail’s overflowing in the box. What if she’s hurt inside? Shouldn’t we call the police or something?”

Roberta’s heart was taking some unnatural beats and she felt the rising panic of being in over her head. “I’m not sure—”

“I’m going to call Kevin, my boyfriend. He works security for concerts and stuff at the Dome. He’s got lots of police friends. He’ll know what to do.”

Roberta made friends with Poochie while Chrissy wandered through the front yard, phone to her ear.

“Okay, the police are on their way,” Chrissy returned.

“But how, exactly, are we going to explain what we’re doing here?”

“Oh, good point. I don’t want my name on anything, my parents still don’t know Liz is missing. I’ll walk down the street and wait there. You can come pick me up when you’re finished.”

“Wait a minute—”

“Just say she’s a friend and she didn’t turn up for a meeting and you got worried. That’s true. Fudge on any details you need to…the pile of papers and mail is enough to warrant some concern, Kevin said. You don’t have to prove anything has really happened.”

“Honestly—” Roberta’s exasperation was interrupted by a voice wafting over the fence.

“Have you come for the dog?”

"Excuse me?" Roberta turned to see an elderly woman on her front porch, a sweater wrapped around her housedress and slippers on her feet.

"I thought maybe you'd come for the dog." The woman came down the steps and approached the fence between the yards. Roberta could see there was a small gap beneath the fence, and that the dog's food bowl and water were stationed there.

"We're—" Roberta suddenly realized Chrissy was nowhere to be seen. "I'm looking for my friend Liz. Have you seen her?"

"Not for several days. I was getting worried, because she's never been gone like this. She asked me to feed the dog over the weekend, which I did, but it's really not like her to leave him for so long. He has a doggie door to get into the house, so all I have to do is put his food right here, but it's still not like her to be gone for so long."

Just then a police car pulled up out front. After a few moments an officer came through the gate, Poochie running circles around him. Roberta explained her concerns about her friend. She was coming to the end of the story when the neighbor interrupted again from the fence.

"I have a key to the house. Would that help?"

Roberta looked at her incredulously. They wouldn't have had to call the police if she'd known the woman had a key. And why hadn't she taken in this week's papers and mail?

The officer took the key and walked to the back. He returned ten minutes later, stating there was no sign of anything out of place. The neighbor reiterated that Liz had in fact been out of town on the weekend, but was supposed to return by Sunday evening. She also had the names of Liz's daughters in Portland in her house, and went back to get them.

All of this was related by Roberta to Tony later that evening. Roberta had decided it was worth making contact with him just to see if he could make sense out of anything that had happened. Although first she had had to recall him on her land line instead of her cell. He didn't care much for cell phones, it turned out.

"So where is the dog now?"

"I have it. Don't ask. The neighbor said it didn't get along with her cats and the poor thing seemed so lonely. He's a nice dog, it's not a problem. I have an old dog who gets along with everyone."

"So she was away over the weekend and didn't come back. And why was Dr. Fleming trying to throw us off the trail? I think he's involved in a very bad way."

"That makes no sense at all."

"Maybe he was cheating on the books and she found out. It's a joint practice, you know. She must have found out something about him."

"You're being ridiculous. The man goes to church—"

"—or *he* found out something about *her*, he was blackmailing her, she confronted him, they argued, there was a fight, and an accidental death."

"Just stop! Have you ever talked to Dr. Fleming for even five minutes??"

"No."

"Well, I started with him. He's the nicest man in the world. He did not harm Liz. And actually, he is technically missing now himself. It's really quite curious. We need to know where Liz went on the weekend to find out why she didn't come back."

"All right, let me work on that. Where can I reach you tomorrow about ten?"

"I'll be at work. I can give you that number if you won't use my cell."

"No, it would be better if you could call me. Can you get on a secure line then? I'll give you a different number."

"Tony, what is all this spy stuff? It's just a phone call."

"Do you want to find her or not?"

"Of course I do. And I'd say you're overdue for an appointment yourself. So give me the number…I'll call you."

Roberta had just hung up the phone when it rang again. The Caller ID came up Donna Noyes.

"Hi, Donna."

"Roberta." Donna had been crying. "I'm sorry to call you. I had your number on my phone. I just didn't know what to do. I thought I'd call to see what you found out today."

"Well, you were right. We found the house and we found her dog, who is now residing in my kitchen. The neighbor said Liz was supposed to be back Sunday night but never returned. Chrissy called the police, so they've taken a report. Tony thinks he might be able to find out where she was—don't ask me how. That man is a little strange."

"That's a lot more than you knew last night." Donna's voice was so quiet Roberta could feel the hurt over the phone.

"You're feeling bad tonight?"

"Awful." Donna was quiet for another minute. "I can't believe how rotten my husband is being. And his family. After all these years that I've worked side by side with them."

"Do you have a good attorney?"

"I think so. He says not to worry, it's all bluff on their part, and it will get worked out in the end. But my husband's saying such awful things about me, and it gets back to my kids. It seems hopeless that I'll ever have a normal life again."

"Are you taking anything?"

"You mean like drugs? Or alcohol?"

"Drugs, I meant. Alcohol definitely won't help."

"I know. But most of those antidepressants end up adding weight. That's already a problem for me."

"But wouldn't it be okay for a while, to feel a little better?"

"Spoken by a woman who has never battled the bulge, I bet."

"No, I made my bargain with the scale years ago. We had a sudden death in the family. I wouldn't have made it without an antidepressant. You can deal with the weight later. It comes off. Not easily, I admit, but it comes off."

"Now you sound just like Liz."

"I'll take that as a compliment. Really, you should think about it if you've been like this for six months. If for no other reason than revenge, I'd think you'd want to be at your best as you go through this divorce."

"Now that's a tactic Liz hasn't tried. Being in good shape to exact the ultimate vengeance. That's good."

"It's probably not listed in the counseling manual. Might have some ethical ramifications."

Donna laughed. "I'll write my own manual, 'Getting even when you're feeling bad…Getting *more* even when you're feeling good.'"

"The title needs some work, but you're getting the idea."

"Thanks, Roberta. I feel better after talking to you. Keep me posted on what happens, okay?"

"Of course."

The next morning Roberta slid into the momentarily empty file room to use the phone.

"I've got it," Tony announced triumphantly. "But I can't tell you on the phone. Can we meet tonight? Maybe at the coffee shop? And we need the others to come, too."

"I don't know, Tony, I was supposed to take my daughters shopping for prom dresses tonight."

"It's really important, and we need to be together to figure out what to do. Could you give me that girl Chrissy's phone number? I'll call her, you get the other woman. Six o'clock, at the coffee shop, okay?"

Roberta wasn't crazy about handing over Chrissy's number, but considering Tony's cell phone phobia she decided it would probably be all right. She put in a call to Donna, left a message at home for the Dents to go shopping without her, then worked the afternoon wondering what the news was going to be.

Although the drive-through lane was backed up around the building, inside the coffee shop things were rather quiet. Tony was sitting in his same seat, back to the wall, watching the front door, when Roberta entered. Donna arrived, still in her baggy sweats and not looking much better. Two minutes later Chrissy came through the door, carrying a medium-sized plastic bag.

"You got them?" Tony asked her. "Let's see."

Chrissy reached in the bag and pulled out a bright red tee-shirt. The words "RAVE FIRST AID" were printed in large letters around a white cross in the middle of the shirt.

"That's it?" Tony was obviously disappointed. "That's the best you could do?"

"It's all I could get," Chrissy apologized. "Kevin works security at the concerts, and they give these out to the volunteers who man the first aid station."

"I was hoping for something that looked more like an official security uniform," Tony replied.

"I know, but Kevin said this was all he could do without outright stealing something. Even these we should give back when we're finished."

"What's going on?" Roberta asked. "Security uniforms? What did you find out?"

Tony hunched over the table conspiratorially. The rest of them leaned in, too.

"It's Mad Cow," he said slowly, waiting to see the effect on their faces.

"Mad Cow?" Roberta repeated, a vision of the happy California cheese cows in her head.

"They think she has Mad Cow and have her holed up at the False Bay Naval Hospital isolation ward. Possibly Dr. Fleming, too. So we have to break them out," Tony spoke as if this were too obvious to even elaborate on.

"Hold on," Roberta objected. "Can you start back a few pages? Something perhaps of this world?"

Tony appeared hurt at the failure of the group to appreciate the immensity of his news. But then social skills had never been his strong point.

"Last weekend, Liz and the doc went to Vancouver for a conference. On Sunday, she became ill. When crossing home at the border, she was detained."

"Because she was sick?" Donna asked.

"Right. Because by this time they had figured out that there had been tainted meat at the conference, and they were in full damage control."

"I do remember seeing something about Mad Cow in the paper this week," Donna said. "But it was pretty minor, one cow in a field in Canada."

"That's all they want you to know," Tony said. "Any hint of Mad Cow in this country would be the biggest blow to agriculture we've ever had. Ever wonder why you never see anything about it in the U.S.? Because they will never, ever admit that we have a problem. You will never see a single case of it identified, you will never hear of a single person having CJD—that's the human form of Bovine Spongiform Encephalopathy. There is a complete conspiracy between the government and the Departments of

Agriculture and Food and Drug that this disease will never be seen in the United States."

"Were you up all night watching Oliver Stone movies or something?" Roberta asked. Chrissy gave her a quizzical look. "Conspiracy theories," Roberta explained. "Everything is a conspiracy."

"Oh, like Mel Gibson in 'Conspiracy Theory?'"

"Something like that. Anyway, that's ridiculous."

"Of course it's ridiculous, because she's a vegetarian," Tony argued. "She never would have eaten the tainted meat anyway."

"No, I meant the whole theory." Roberta's head was beginning to pound and she was sorry she hadn't ordered something super caffeinated before she sat down. "Tony—"

"Look, believe me or not. I can't tell you how I have the information, I just have it. I know a lot of people. I can get information when I need to. Things are not always what they seem. So believe me or not, I don't care. But I'm going to figure out a way to get her back."

"He's right that she's a vegetarian," Chrissy said, breaking what was becoming an awkward silence. "She told me that once."

"See?" Tony looked pointedly at Roberta.

"I do remember now that she was going to a conference last weekend. She said something about being worried about the lines at the border with the new security. I completely forgot about it until you mentioned it," Donna said.

Tony looked at Roberta again.

"Okay, okay. She was out of the country for a conference, and she's a vegetarian, and there was something about Mad Cow in Canada last week. I'm with you up to that point. Even if she got some kind of food poisoning, why would she be at False Bay? And why all the secrecy?"

"Because it's Mad Cow," Tony said in exasperation. "They have to keep it quiet. They have to keep them isolated. No one can know about it, so that means no regular hospitals. So that means military. The only nearby military base with a completely safe isolation room is at False Bay…because they're prepared for any nuclear accidents they might have."

Roberta sighed. "So you think that the Canadian government and the U.S. government have conspired together to hold two U.S. citizens hostage on an isolated military base because they might have eaten tainted meat in Vancouver."

"Exactly," Tony was obviously pleased that she had finally figured it out. "Now how shall we get them out?"

"But if she's sick, shouldn't she stay there?" Donna asked.

"She's *not* sick, she's a vegetarian, remember? She probably has some flu bug or something. They could hold her forever and who would know about it?"

"Well, her daughters and the police are starting to look for her. Won't that be a problem?" Donna asked.

"And what about Dr. Fleming? Or is he a vegetarian, too?"

"I don't have confirmation on that," Tony replied, completely missing Roberta's sarcasm. "To be honest, I can't confirm that they are together, although it seems logical since he's missing, too. And within days, her daughters and the police will receive some information that will make them call off the search. That she decided to take a short vacation and she's perfectly all right. Meanwhile, she'll be locked up at False Bay."

"So what do you suggest, Tony?" Roberta thought humoring him for a moment might give her time to think of some way to get them all out of this.

"I suggest driving up and breaking her out. They won't be expecting it, so we'll have the element of surprise. But I was hoping for the uniforms…we need something official looking."

"I have a white van you can use," Donna said. "It doesn't have any markings on it, and the windows are dark…you know, it protects the flowers. It might look official."

"Donna, you can't really go along with this." Roberta stared at her incredulously.

"I need her back," Donna's eyes filled with tears. "I'll do anything."

"I can't go with you. But maybe I could ask if Kevin has any ideas." Chrissy tried to be helpful.

"I think this whole thing is a crock," Roberta said.

"I didn't want it to come to this," Tony reached into the briefcase beside him and pulled out a small laptop. "I don't like logging on in public places. But I'm going to bring up a couple of web sites for you. If, after reading them, you still don't believe me, then okay, we'll forget the whole thing. But if you have even an inkling that it might be true, you have to promise to help. Deal?"

"Fine. First I'm going over for a venti triple-shot latte. Then I'll look at it."

And so the following day Roberta found herself calling in sick to work and driving north in the white van with Tony and Donna, the three of them dressed in the scrubs Roberta had snuck into work on Thursday night and taken under the guise of repairing torn hems. *This is the most ridiculous thing I have ever done,* she thought. And yet, Tony's evidence had seemed convincing yesterday. But today, a familiar small panic was beginning in her chest. She was the driver, and she tried to simply concentrate on the road.

"Tony, since I am putting myself in some peril with you today, do you mind telling me where you got your information about Liz getting picked up at the border?

Who do you know who would have access to that information?"

"I can't say, I'm sorry."

"Let's see, what are the possibilities? Ex-military. Ex-FBI. Ex-CIA. Homeland Security. Witness Protection." Roberta noticed a flinch in Tony's hand when she got to Witness Protection. "That's it, huh? Witness Protection? But you've still got some contacts, some handlers or something? Something happened back East and you were relocated out here?"

"Not exactly."

"And they try to keep you happy so when you come up with a crazy story like this they just go along with it?"

"I don't think it's that crazy," Donna put in from the back seat.

It seemed crazier and crazier to Roberta with each mile she drove. But, what the heck, she wanted Liz back, too, and she'd do just about anything to find her.

Three hours later, the white van with its darkened windows and one very large flower arrangement in the back made the turn at the False Bay sign. Within a quarter mile she could see the first gatehouse.

"I can't do this," she whispered to Tony.

"Of course you can. Take a deep breath right now. Pretend you're playing a role in a movie. This is important. We have to get through the first gate."

It was over before Roberta even had time to finish rolling down her window. The guard simply refused them entry, refused to take the belatedly offered flowers, and directed Roberta to back up and turn around. He pointed to the video cameras one time to get his point across and read to her the complete registration information about the van, obviously gleaned instantaneously from the license plate and displayed on his computer as she drove up to the gate. Thank God the van was registered to the Noyes flower business, and they did at least have flowers. But the guard was having none of it, and sternly but politely repeated that there was no access and she would need to turn around. Then he watched her intently as she hesitantly put the van in reverse.

No one said a word. Roberta didn't even realize how much she had been sweating until they were back on the main road and she felt a little trickle of dampness at the back of her neck. She loosened her jacket.

"I guess it was worth a shot," she finally said. "I don't know how we thought we were just going to waltz in there, anyway. It's a nuclear missile base, for heaven's sakes. They probably get all sorts of crazy people trying to get in." Her own words reverberated in her brain as she considered her situation: two women and one man dressed in medical office scrubs in a nursery van with a floral bouquet requesting permission to enter the base. *How did I get talked into this??*

They drove thirty miles in silence. Roberta was pondering the mess that was her life at the moment when her cell phone rang so suddenly and loudly that she startled and accidentally sent the van into the shoulder lane. "Sorry!" she recovered. "Tony, could you look in my purse and see who it is? I can't talk and drive."

Tony fumbled through her purse and got the phone up after two more rings. His face broke into a broad smile.

"It's Liz!" he announced, reading the Caller ID. "Hello, Roberta's phone," he answered in a neutral voice. "Yes, it's me. She's driving and can't talk. It's good to hear your voice."

"Let me talk to her, oh, please, let me talk to her before you hang up," Donna cried from the back seat.

"Yes, we're having a little trip, thought we might come find you. Really…well, that's good that you're feeling better. Dr. Fleming was a bit confused, you know."

Roberta was dying to hear the other side of the conversation, and almost asked for the phone. Now Tony was relaying to her directly.

"She says she spoke to her daughter and thank you so much for taking care of the dog. She won't be back home until tonight, but you can take the dog over any time today and leave it, he'll be fine."

"Please—" Donna was nearly whimpering in the back seat.

"Listen, there's someone else here who wants to talk to you," Tony handed the phone back to Donna. The conversation was lost in Donna's tearful weeping.

"So where's she been?" Roberta asked Tony.

"She said she got sick coming home from the conference, and she's been in a hospital near the border, and there was a mix-up with the neighbor who's getting a little senile. She said we can all call her tonight." A happy grin spread over his face as he looked out the window.

"What are you so happy about?" Roberta asked. "We just wasted a whole afternoon and a tank full of gas."

He looked at her in surprise. "What do you mean? We saved her!"

"What are you talking about? We never even saw her."

"They knew we were there and we knew she was there. They had to let her go."

Roberta managed to tear her eyes from the road long enough to look at him in disbelief. "Are you nuts?"

Tony was wounded. "You don't find it highly suspicious that within one half-hour of our arrival at the gate, we had a phone call from someone we've been trying to get in touch with for four days? How do you explain that?"

"Coincidence. She's probably been calling all her clients. She just finally got to me."

"You can think what you want, then. But I guarantee you, if we hadn't made this trip, you wouldn't be sitting in your favorite chair in her office by Monday afternoon."

Roberta gripped the steering wheel. The man was crazy, that's all there was to it. And hopefully, hopefully harmless. She sent up a little prayer to that effect.

Donna had finished her conversation and passed the phone back up to Tony.

"Thank you so much. I can't tell you how much better I feel just knowing she's okay. She said to call tonight and we can set up appointments for Monday, or tomorrow, if anyone is desperate."

"You didn't tell her what we were doing, did you?" Roberta asked carefully.

"No, when she asked why we were together I just said we'd met Monday while waiting in her office. I'm so relieved." Donna started to cry again.

"You've *got* to get on some antidepressants," Roberta said, not unkindly.

"Better living through chemicals," Tony concurred.

"I'll think about," Donna sniffled. "Honest. Maybe I'll give them a try. Like you said, Roberta, to be in the best shape to exact revenge."

Tony smiled approvingly. "Now there's a motto."

It was Monday at noon. Roberta had entered the empty office and then wandered back to Liz's door. Liz was just hanging up her phone and waved her in. Roberta sank into her favorite spot, the end of the couch where she could lean on the arm and tuck her feet beneath her if she wanted. Liz smiled warmly. Roberta honestly wanted to jump up and hug her, but their relationship was more professional than that.

"I hear you went on a rescue mission for me. I'm very flattered."

"Did you hear the part about Chrissy making out like a bandit while you were gone? She's the only one who got ahead in all this."

"I appreciate the thought, but I was perfectly all right. Just down with the flu for a few days in Canada, in the hospital, actually, and my poor neighbor got things rather botched up. And apparently Dr. Fleming had a family emergency of his own, but of course I had no idea. I could only make one call before I became violently ill, and I needed to make sure my neighbor would keep feeding the dog. Thank you so much for taking him."

"It was no problem. Things just spiraled out of control, somehow. Tony is certainly an interesting character. I can't imagine being in Witness Protection…" *Wait, what had just passed on Liz's face? Had she raised her eyebrows almost imperceptibly? Her face that never revealed a single thing that she was really thinking, no matter how shocking your confessions or boring your lamentations... OH, no!* "He's not in Witness Protection, is he? All the cloak and dagger stuff, the land lines, the secrecy, he's just a crazy paranoid."

"You know I can't talk about my other clients." *Oh, she is so smooth.* "Let's talk about how you've been these two weeks. What's new with the Dents? And the older girls?"

Roberta sighed. She leaned her head back against the couch for a moment and closed her eyes. It would be okay. Everything would be okay now. It didn't matter that Tony had nearly set them up for imprisonment or worse. It didn't matter that she had lied about taking home three sets of scrubs, especially since she really did re-hem them just so she wouldn't be lying. She was in her favorite spot, with her favorite person after her husband across from her, and she would probably never see Tony or Donna or Chrissy again. Life would go back to its rhythm, and every week for a little while she would have this oasis of time in this pleasant place, where she could try to figure out why her life was off-kilter despite so many blessings, where she could learn to understand why sometimes the waves seemed too big.

"It's the twins causing the uproar this week," she began. "They've both declared they want to move back home and get jobs and save money while they decide about graduate school. The nest might not be so empty after all."

And just putting that thought into words made her feel a little bit better.

Chapter Two: Edwinna Scissorhands

June—November, 2011

The woman was dressed completely in black from her cap pulled low to her gloves and boots. She had even darkened her face. The only clue she was crouched beside the bush at the edge of the park was the glint of the streetlight reflecting off the sharp pruning shears in her hand as she reached out to trim the offending branches.

How many times had she sat in her car at the nearby corner, unable to see oncoming traffic because of this bush? But with ten quick snips, all was improved. She gathered the leafy branches that had fallen to her feet and stuffed them into the black garbage bag she had brought along. Shoving in the last sharp tips she gathered the top of the bag together and made her way back to her car, strategically parked one block away on the darkest part of that street.

It had all started innocently enough. Her mother had taught her years ago how to make that sharp pinch between thumb and forefinger to remove a dead pansy and how easy it was to maintain the roses by quick clipping on a daily basis. Walking through her garden in the late afternoon after a day of teaching middle schoolers in the throes of their adolescent angst, monitoring the garden had become a "regaining sanity hour" before she took on the evening parenting duties for her own teenage sons.

Then a year ago, things had escalated. She had been on her early morning walk, taken an hour before her two boys would begin to stir, and there it was in front of her: a twig which hadn't been there the day before, hanging low over the sidewalk after the previous night's rain, right in her path and ready to rake wetly across her forehead with its sharp wood edges and drops of rain still attached.

So Edwinna MacDonald had reached up and with her expert fingers, simply snapped it off. It was such a small twig that it easily gave way beneath her thumb and forefinger, so practiced at keeping her garden plants tidy. And there was so much downfall from the storm that one more small twig landing on the sidewalk wasn't even noticeable.

But something about this event, the trimming of something that was not technically hers, even though it hung low over a public sidewalk, released a sense of euphoria. A clean, right feeling overcame her, and suddenly she was noticing all sorts of things that needed trimmed which she had never noticed before. And most of them were on property that belonged to other people.

She had gone on this way for an entire year: nightly forays two or three times a week, improving her environment in the smallest ways. She pulled off invasive ivy from the park trees, one tree at a time. She cut bamboo from where it shouldn't be growing, pulled weeds from parking strips, and once, in the middle of a small storm, sawed the dead limb from a street tree that had been bothering her for months. Her collection of sharp and efficient tools was growing. Happily, her sons never ventured into her garden shed to discover the new shears, loppers, and tree saws that kept turning up there. By the end of the year, she could drive to work without running into any bad corners where poorly planted bushes obscured the view of cars or pedestrians. Her neighborhood walk could be completed without a single tree or wild blackberry bush catching her about the head, and no English ivy waiting to grab her ankle and trip her.

But then new things began to bother her. She was an English teacher, so grammar mattered. She tried to ignore the intentional misspellings, created to draw attention to the advertised item: Lo Prices!, Skool Supplies!, Fone Cards! But the day the hand-scribbled "Hot Bagles Here!" sign went up on the coffee stand halfway to work, she simply couldn't let it alone. A search of the teacher's supply room had found paper nearly the same size and color, and with a quick foray out in the middle of the night, the offensive sign was replaced with a properly spelled one: "Hot Bagels Here!" She wondered how an entire generation of young people could have missed so many basic spelling and grammar rules, as she carefully fixed signs that announced, “You’re best buy in town!” or “Its finally here!” And not just the hand-printed signs at the little coffee stands needed fixing. Many small shop owners seemingly had not taken seventh grade English very seriously.

Once she had most of the reachable signs in the area fixed, she started in on the graffiti. She probably could have simply gone to her small local police department and asked to create a graffiti brigade with the city’s blessing, but something about donning her dark outfit and stealing out in the middle of the night had become part of the excitement. She researched the proper paints to use and slowly, slowly, slowly, beautified her town one small splash of paint at a time.

And now she had graduated to her biggest project yet. After spending weeks on surveillance at the local grocery store where the parking lot stalls had disappeared into oblivion and the cart catchers were always in disarray, she had decided to repaint the lines, one section at a time, with quick drying paint. All that was required was the quick sweep of a section with a broom to remove the small gravel and loose dirt, and then a steady hand in applying the bright new yellow stripes with a four-inch, heavy-duty roller. The grocery was closed overnight from midnight to six. By painting at two a.m., the paint was dry by morning. She had started in the darkest corner of the lot, far from the light standards by the front door; two sections were finished and she was nearly half-way done.

On the night in question, Edwinna had stood admiring six freshly repainted stalls when she was startled by a police cruiser pulling around from the back of the store, lights ablaze. She froze, but then relaxed as she saw who it was. Officer Sam had occasionally caught her in the act during her nightly wanderings through their small town, but he had never done more than make her stop and watch her leave.

Giving a slight nod of his head to the other side of the car, Officer Sam pulled his elongated frame from the driver's side. Edwinna watched curiously as he pulled out his big flashlight in an uncharacteristic way, flashing it at her hand holding the paint roller and then over the newly painted surface.

"What are you doing, Ma'am?" he asked sternly.

Edwinna strained to see into the patrol car in the dark, and then the passenger door opened and an officer she didn't know stepped out. Stunned to speechlessness, she was unable to articulate any good story, even though she usually had one practiced for each middle-of-the night excursion.

"Put down the roller, Ma'am," the other officer said brusquely, still standing behind the protection of his open door. Edwinna could not even get out a comedic response asking if he feared he was going to be attacked with yellow paint.

"We had a call from the security guard about possible malicious mischief and destruction of property," Officer Sam said. "Can you tell us what you're doing here?"

"I need to call my lawyer," Edwinna finally managed. And with that her paint was confiscated and she was escorted into the patrol unit.

Her attorney was one of her closest childhood friends, a woman who had firmly guided her through the divorce from the boys' father five years ago and protected her financial interests when Edwinna herself had barely been able to leave her bed. A compassionate woman with an excellent reputation, Judith Cisneros thought she had seen most everything, yet she was unprepared for her client's 3:30 a.m. call from the police station saying she had been arrested for repainting the lines in the grocery store parking lot.

It didn't take much wrangling with the district attorney, a divorced mother herself, to get a plea bargain that would leave nothing on Edwinna's record if she completed counseling, 300 hours of community service, and paid a $2000 fine. If she stayed out of trouble for two years the record would be expunged, and her teaching career would be untainted.

Judith might have even gotten a little less, but she was worried about her friend and thought the counseling and community service might help fill whatever void Edwinna seemed to be trying to satisfy by creating her personal Lady Bird Johnson Beautification program. The district attorney had understood completely about not giving any ammunition to the boys' father, not that he would try to challenge the 25-75 custody agreement, but you could never be sure when an attack of fatherly guilt might take place. So everything was done as quietly as possible and three weeks later Edwinna found herself sitting across from Dr. Mark Fleming, her court-appointed counselor.

He looked a little young to be an experienced counselor, Edwinna decided immediately. She was expecting someone more Freud-like, bearded and old. Dr. Fleming was nice looking, of average height, and wore dark-rimmed glasses which added that trustworthy look. She supposed he could be forty or so.

"What would you like to be called?" he inquired kindly. "You can call me Mark."

"Edwinna will be fine," she mumbled, feeling like one of her recalcitrant students, called before the class for some awkward offense such as note-passing or spit balls.

"Would you like to start at the beginning? Tell me how you came to be repainting the lines in the grocery parking lot in the middle of the night?"

Not really, she thought. But the dangling carrot of a clean record and no harm to her teaching certification prompted her to at least be civil. She glanced around the office walls trying to organize her thoughts. A small sign to the left of the calming woodland photographs caught her eye: Tears Welcome. Hmm. She had not cried since the day the divorce was final, the day she buried all her feelings in the concrete safe of her heart and threw away the key.

She started at the beginning, with the little snips of wayward twigs when she was out walking, then the escalation to trimming the poorly placed bushes to improve visibility at intersections, to fixing the grammatically challenged signs, to covering the graffiti, and finally her grand idea to repaint the parking lot.

Dr. Fleming listened quietly, no hint of surprise or judgmental disapproval on his face, though she was sure he was suppressing a smile when she got to the part about the police officer hiding behind his car door.

When she finished, he sat thoughtfully for a moment, then asked, "When you say these things 'bothered' you, what do you mean? Did they make you feel anxious? Or angry?"

Edwinna thought about it, then tried to explain how at first it had been for necessity but then had spilled over into some kind of neat-and-tidy desire.

"Have you developed any other new habits? Excessive hand-washing? Cleaning your house more often? Only able to use certain pens or pencils at school?"

Well, of course, I have to use a red pen at school. But she got his point.

"I don't think I'm obsessive-compulsive, if that's where you're going," she replied. And yet, it *was* nearly impossible not to snip off a dead pansy head if she passed a neglected plant.

"After your divorce—"

Oh, golly, here we go, the divorce,

"—did you have time to process the changes in your life, or did you have to keep your nose to the grindstone, you know, keep on teaching school, raising the boys, keeping up the house?"

"I didn't get two months off to go to a wellness retreat center and contemplate my failures, if that's what you mean," Edwinna said. "Life went on."

"What was the boys' reaction?"

"To the divorce?"

"Oh, no, sorry, I meant to your arrest."

"The oldest one is terribly embarrassed, even though it was kept quiet. The younger one is a little more supportive."

"How does that line up with their feelings about the divorce?"

"About the same, I guess."

"And your work? Teaching middle school these days is terribly stressful. You've been teaching how long?"

"Eighteen years. Eight before our first son was born, then ten since I went back after they were both in elementary."

"And you've seen some big changes since you first started teaching. That would have been when…in the early 80's?"

Edwinna wanted to leave. She hated talking about work. She hated teaching. She hated the kids, who arrived late smelling of alcohol or dope, never did their homework but had their parents emailing daily about why they weren't getting A's. She hated their sense of privilege and their lack of respect for their elders. She hated all of it.

"Edwinna?"

Not realizing she'd been quiet for so long, Edwinna was embarrassed that a lump had formed in her throat and she had to blink to keep tears from forming.

"This is obviously touching on some deep feelings for you. So perhaps work is the first sticking point. Somehow it is not fulfilling you the way it used to."

Edwinna nodded, refusing to let any tears come.

"I've heard this from a lot of teachers, lately. Education used to be held in such high regard. Parents demanded their children respect their teachers and do their homework. Now, there's little help from the home front…you're expected to do it all and get every kid into a four-year university, too."

"And pass the state tests along the way," Edwinna said softly.

"Oh, right. You've got seventh grade?"

"And one eighth grade Advanced English class."

"Which at one time was probably a bright spot but now...all the parents want their kids to go to Harvard?"

"Stanford, actually."

"Hmm. So where once your work was a chance to inspire and use your creativity in positive ways, now it's—"

"Hell."

"So your forays into the night to straighten up the world are where you get your positives. When you pass by the intersection that you clipped the night before, how do you feel?"

"I like it. I like that the view is not obstructed. Or if there were low bushes straggling out that were going to trip someone, I like seeing that they're neat and tidy behind the sidewalk."

"A sense of order."

"Yes."

"And painting the parking lot?"

"I couldn't stand it anymore." Edwinna rolled her eyes. "I shop there four times a week to keep enough food in the house for the boys, and the lines haven't been repainted for years. Cars were parking every which way. No one observed the handicapped stalls, the basket catchers were pulled apart. There was no reason for it. It just needed some paint."

"Simply making a request to the management didn't cross your mind?"

Edwinna shrugged. "There was something about effecting change in the middle of the night, of no one knowing, of a grand surprise. No one noticed the other things I did. I guess I was ready for a big one."

"I think you're ready to have your efforts noticed and appreciated." Dr. Fleming turned the page of his writing pad. "You have an awful lot to offer the world, so let's get your priorities reoriented, shall we?"

Edwinna looked at the carpet.

"It's not going to be painful, I promise," Dr. Fleming said sympathetically. "You have closed yourself off a bit, and we're going to open that door. Here's what I'd suggest. You've got 300 hours of community service to do. My church hosts a dinner on Wednesday nights. I'd like you to start volunteering there, from 5-9. That'll knock off four hours a week, and that's a good start. Or do you have a church of your own? Or perhaps volunteer opportunities somewhere else you'd prefer?"

"I stopped going to church after the divorce. They always wanted me to teach the middle school Sunday morning class...just what I wanted to do after a week of the little darlings."

"All right then, Wednesday night, here's the address," he pulled a card out of his desk drawer. "Show up and they'll tell you what to do."

"Okay."

"For the rest of this week, I want you to keep a journal. It can be a short one, but each day after dinner, write down three things that made you feel good and three things that made you angry or depressed."

"I might have trouble coming up with the three good things."

"It can be as easy as the car started on the first attempt. But three things."

"Okay, I'll try."

"I'll see you next week, then. Bring your journal with you. Oh, and lock your clippers and paint brushes in the garage so you won't be tempted."

"Right."

Three weeks later, Edwinna dragged herself from the car through the back door of her house. Pulling off her work boots, she put her sun hat on its hook and took the hair band out of her hair, letting the long strands fall down for the first time since morning. Every part of her body ached. It was only the third day of her new summer job, taken to help pay off the $2000 fine. Two thousand dollars she had taken from the boys' college fund, money that would be needed when Paul, a senior in high school, started submitting his college applications in the fall.

Upstairs in her room, she closed the door, and started the water running into the master bathtub. She pulled off her overalls and long sleeved, sun-protective work shirt, pulled her hair back up on her head, and tested the water: It was approaching perfection. Slipping into the tub, she lay back against the end, letting the warm stream from the spigot pour over her tired feet.

Her attorney had been the one who had a friend who knew someone whose sister owned a small gardening business, and it hadn't taken too much to get hired on as a summer worker. Pay was only a little above minimum wage, and Edwinna was by far the oldest of the part-time help. Thankfully, there were several strong young people who could haul the heaviest bags of bark and soil. She did her share of lifting and shoveling, though, and every muscle in her body was feeling it tonight. Judith's thought must have been that she would enjoy working with plants in an organized, legal manner, but, in fact, at this point it was pretty much just a job. There wasn't much excitement in covering a slope with small plantings or packing a huge ceramic pot with annuals. But it was income, and it was keeping her asleep at night instead of being up wandering the streets.

After her bath, she pulled on her most comfortable jeans and a tee-shirt and went downstairs to start dinner. Taped to the little countertop television in the kitchen was a note from the boys…they would be out for the evening, "don't wait up." She sighed, knowing she would have to track them down on their cell phones to get the details. They were taking advantage of her absence to slide out before she had done her daily inquisitions of their evening plans, but she was hoping that after enough embarrassing phone calls from her they'd get the message and start leaving more complete itineraries.

The mail was strewn on the counter-top. She flipped through the envelopes quickly. The cable bill, the phone bill and, *hmm, what was this one*, a business envelope from the grocery.

As she unfolded the letter within, a check fell to the floor. She picked it up and turned it over…made out to her, for $500, from corporate headquarters. She examined it again to see if it was some kind of gimmick or fake come-on. She looked at the letter. Signed by the manager of her local store it thanked her for her efforts to make repairs to the parking lot. Short and simple.

Edwinna's face broke into a broad smile, then a happy laugh, then she ran around the kitchen and shrieked with joy as she waved the check above her head. The manager felt badly about her arrest; he had told her several times that the security guard had acted on his own when calling the police.

Five hundred dollars! It would take her at least two weeks at the landscaping job to bring home that much after all the taxes were taken out of her paychecks. Things were looking up.

Edwinna was dreading the start of the new school year. Thank goodness her arrest had taken place after school was out, but surely news would leak and be remembered, in September.

Maybe it would have been better to be in jail this fall, Edwinna pondered as she carried a load of the boys' jeans to the washing machine. She sighed. Tonight was Wednesday, and she needed to start her service hours. Her attorney had stressed that showing her cooperation and repentance in all areas was extremely important.

Edwinna pulled her own clean clothes from the dryer, put the boys' whites from the washer into the dryer and started it, and then filled the tub in preparation for the jeans. She carried the basket of laundry to her bed and dumped it, contemplating what to wear that evening. Kakis and a cotton top, she decided; an old one that could withstand dish duty for several hours.

Edwinna arrived at the church about ten minutes early. She had passed the small Lutheran church many times on her way to school, and had even noticed the sign outside about Wednesday night community dinners. Finding her way to the social hall and kitchen, Edwinna introduced herself to a tall woman in an apron with a spoon in her hand who was directing the setting up of tables and looked like she was in charge.

"Oh, yes, Mark said you might be coming by. We're so happy to have the extra help, especially this month when people are on vacation. I'm Marge."

Edwinna observed the number of chairs being set out.

"How many do you serve each week?"

"It varies, a hundred to a hundred and fifty."

Edwinna's forehead furrowed in amazement.

"It's always a shock the first time people come. No one ever thinks there's poverty in the suburbs. But right now, for families on that thin line, one free meal a week might mean they can afford their medicine or gas for the car or a monthly insurance payment."

"I guess that's right," Edwinna thought about the amount of food her own boys ate. "Well, what would you like me to do?"

"There are some paper placemats on the counter in the kitchen. You could put them out. We've found it makes things a little more cheerful to have some color on the tables. Hey, everyone," Marge turned around and yelled to the rest of the kitchen, "here's our new helper," she hesitated, and Edwinna could tell she was struggling to remember the right name.

"Edwinna," she helped her along.

"Edwinna!" Marge finished. "Do you have a nickname or anything?"

"Not really."

"All right, Edwinna it is. Hey, Donna?" Marge called to a shorter, dark-haired woman in sweat pants who was working on the table set up. "Could you please show Edwinna here the ropes?"

"Glad to," Donna replied. "Grab those placemats and I'll show you where to start."

The rest of the evening went by quickly. By the time all the tables and chairs were set up, it was nearly six o'clock. The doors opened at 6:15. Edwinna took a spot beside Donna on the chow line, helping to ladle up a good-smelling stew. Then she took a turn circulating with the baskets of rolls, and finally did some clearing and Donna showed her how to use the dishwasher. She had never considered herself uninformed, and she certainly had taught many students whose families were struggling, but she was overwhelmed with the number of people who arrived, especially those with young children in tow.

The next Wednesday evening things were more familiar, and Edwinna had a chance to look closely at the crowd. She recognized three of her students from the previous year, but they kept a wide berth and ate together at a table away from their families. There was a row of older men that Donna said took a bus out from town because they liked what the church served better than what was offered at their own shelter. There were several tables of mothers with young kids. One mom was trying to feed a toddler while she held a crying baby, and Edwinna went by and offered to hold the little one. She had forgotten the warm, pleasant feeling of a diapered bottom in a cotton onesie, the soft little legs pressing against her arm and the big eyes searching her face, trying to decide whether to let out another wail or not. Edwinna gently bounced the baby in a rhythm and slowly backed away so the baby couldn't hear her mom's voice. To her surprise, the baby quieted as she crooned, eventually falling asleep. Now Edwinna's arm felt as if it might break. Sawing tree limbs was one thing, holding twelve pounds of dead weight in an awkward position was another.

At their next session, Dr. Fleming noticed that she had brightened considerably when talking about the dinners.

"I liked holding that baby, I have to admit," Edwinna told him. Calculating how many years it might be before she had grandchildren of her own, the answer had been in double digits.

"Good. This is good," Dr. Fleming smiled.

At the end of a Wednesday evening in September, Edwinna noticed a teen boy by the large, wall-mounted automatic coffee pots, struggling to get the lid off. He looked vaguely familiar. She asked if Donna knew his name, and when she didn't, Edwinna walked over.

"Can I give you a hand?" she asked.

The boy turned around. "Oh, Mrs. Mac! I saw you but I wasn't sure it was you."

Edwinna ran through all the names she could think of, but none of them were fitting.

"I'm Julio. You don't remember me because I never had you for class. But you had my older brother Javier."

"Oh, of course. No wonder you looked familiar. How nice of you to volunteer here."

Julio looked a bit sheepish.

"Actually, it's community service for the ninth grade school requirement this year. I needed a place I could walk to cause I don't drive yet."

"Well, here, let me see if I can get the top off for you." Edwinna stood on her tip toes so she could read the raised letters on the black cap to see which way it said "Twist to open." Then it still took both of them together to budge the lid.

"Why didn't I ever have you in class?" Edwinna asked as they poured the last of the coffee into the sink. "I teach all the seventh grade English classes."

"I didn't take your class."

"Everyone takes seventh grade English." The coffee steam filled the air around them.

"I had to take the other class cause my English isn't that good."

Edwinna was confused, but then realized he must be talking about the English Language Learner class. Yet the students there were mostly newly arrived kids with very poor oral English.

"You mean the ELL class? That doesn't make any sense, Julio, your English is excellent. And your family has been here for a long time, I thought."

"Well, it was really good to see you, Mrs. Mac. I gotta go, be home by 9:00." And with that he was gone.

Something nagged at the back of Edwinna's brain for the entire week, and it must have resolved itself in a dream because the next Tuesday morning she woke up and knew what she had to do. After school, she dropped into the World Languages classroom and spoke with her friend. When she left, Edwinna had a neatly printed letter in Spanish in her coat pocket.

On Wednesday night, Julio was volunteering again, and at the end of the evening Edwinna found him.

"Julio, I'm so glad to see you. I was hoping you could help me. I got this letter from a former student, but it's in Spanish and I can't read it." She pulled out the short note and handed it to him. She was absolutely certain she recognized the first look of fear on his face before the coping strategies engaged.

"'Dear Mrs. Mac, I'm having a good time here in Guatemala on my vacation. Wish you were here.' But I can't read that signature."

"Okay, thanks."

When Edwinna got home she called her friend. "He can't read Spanish, either. Not a clue what the letter really said, except 'Guatemala.'"

"Well, that would explain why he was in the ELL class, I guess. You said you taught his brother, how did he do?"

"I can't remember, which means he must have been okay. Wasn't falling out the bottom, anyway."

"Then I think you might be right, Julio must have a reading disability. It's a shame, he's a nice kid. He came to the environmental club meetings for a while, but he didn't stick with it. And now that I think of it, once the kids started doing so much research online, that's when he quit coming."

It took two more Wednesdays before Edwinna felt comfortable bringing up reading skills with Julio. By then they had spent plenty of time on the dish scraping line together. Julio was unchaining his bike from the stand outside the church when Edwinna was leaving.

"Julio, I want to ask you something, and I hope I won't offend you. But I've been wondering if the reason you weren't in my English class is because you've got some trouble reading English. It's certainly not your spoken English that is the problem."

"Yeah, I've never been able to read English well."

"And what about Spanish?"

There was a long pause. Julio got the final numbers and gave his lock a jerk.

"I'm not so good at reading, Mrs. Mac, I'm stupid that way."

"No, no, Julio, that's what I'm trying to figure out. I think you have what's called a reading disability. Some kids can learn everything else just fine, but they can't make sense of reading. Is there anyone else in your family who has trouble reading?"

"My dad's just like me. He and my mom have a car shop, but she does all the written work. He's good with people, good with math and good with his hands, but he's always blamed his trouble on the English. But one time, when I was little, my mom told me, I'm just like him. It doesn't matter which language."

"Well, I have an idea if you're willing. I have a friend who could work with you, give you a couple tests, and maybe that would help us know a better way to teach you. I'd really like to help you learn to read. Especially this year, before you have to take the written driver's license test. Would you be willing?"

"Nah, nothing will help. My mom tried and tried."

"But that's because she didn't know what's making it hard."

It took some convincing, but by the beginning of October, Edwinna was sitting in the school counselor's office reviewing Julio's test results.

"He's weak in visual memory and discrimination. He can't tell the difference between letters, and has a really hard time remembering things he's only seen visually. In English and Spanish both. You'll need a really strong auditory approach to teach him to read."

"But which language should we start in?" Edwinna wondered.

"Do you speak Spanish?"

"No."

"Then I guess you'll be starting in English."

And so began Mrs. Edwinna Scissorhand's After School Program for Non-Readers. When school opened in September, the kids gave Edwinna the 'Scissorhand' nickname as soon as the stories of her nightly wanderings and arrest spread.

The reading program started with Julio and grew to over twenty-five middle and high school students by December, with adult volunteers organized by the middle school librarian, for whom literacy was an undying passion. Somehow the emphasis on learning to read the state driver's test manual had been the spark that made the whole thing go. There were even a few parents who came to the sessions, which expanded to five afternoons a week. Oddly, Edwinna's oldest son Paul, possibly because he was now a senior and senior pranks had become the main topic of conversation among his friends, had not only forgiven Edwinna for causing him embarrassment but had taken a new pride in her accomplishments, those both legal, and not so much.

As she described the growth of her program, Dr. Fleming became curious and stopped by to update her progress for the court. Soon he was in attendance once a week, seated in a comfortable corner chair, students at first shy to go talk with him. Edwinna watched from across the room and liked the ease he had with these teenagers, so many of whom seemed to feel the weight of the world on their young shoulders.

"Hey, Donna," Edwinna looked up from the table where she was tutoring Julio to see her friend from the Wednesday evening dinners peeking through the library door. "What brings you here?"

"Everyone's been talking about how successful your program is. I thought I'd drop by. Think any of your kids might need help with math?"

"Well, yeah, that would be great. Thanks."

Edwinna stood and addressed the group. "Hey, everyone, say hello to Donna Noyes, at our service for math tutoring and small business expertise."

By the end of the fall, the after school program was offering free legal advice by Edwinna's attorney, counseling support from Dr. Fleming, math tutoring led by Donna, and reading help from the librarian's volunteers.

Observing the beehive of activity around her the Tuesday before Thanksgiving break, Edwinna felt two emotions rise in her chest that had been absent for some time: genuine happiness, and pride in her work.

Catching her eye as he listened to a tearful student in his counseling corner, Dr. Fleming gave her the slightest nod.

Edwinna smiled, her fingers neatly pinching off a dead leaf from the librarian's African violet beside her.

Chapter Three: Donna

July—November, 2011

Donna awkwardly tried to stretch her neck while still holding the phone crunched between her ear and shoulder as her hands deftly stripped green leaves from day lily stems and applied water tubes to their ends.

"Yes, I know," she murmured empathetically to the hyperventilating bride who was having yet another meltdown, this time over the hydrangeas for the table centerpieces at the reception which was now three weeks away. "The cold weather *has* been a problem for the local growers. But I promise you, I will have hydrangeas in your color palate of blues and purples by then. I have two back-up plans…everything is covered. Really."

Donna took the phone in her hand and glanced at the clock in her garage office. Day-old rolls and salad fixings for the Wednesday night dinner at her church weren't getting any younger as they waited for her at the grocery.

"Yes, I'll call at the beginning of next week. Everything will be fine. I'm sorry but I have to go now." The new proprietor of "I Do Wedding Flowers" sighed, wondering once again if she had chosen the right field. But somehow "I Do Funeral Flowers" didn't have quite the same appeal.

Half-an-hour later, Donna hurried down the store aisle, her cart overflowing with cellophane bags of small breads and her mind on the other items she needed to pick up. She made a blind turn and came up short as her cart banged into another. When she looked up, she was staring at Tony Wagner.

"Hello, Donna," he said politely.

"Tony! I haven't seen you since—"

"—our adventure to False Bay."

"Right. Sorry I bumped into you. I was rushing. Hope there was no damage, I'm low on cart insurance right now."

"That's all right. It's nice to see you again. Things good with you?"

"Yup. Had to change my day and time with Liz. I've started a home-based business."

"I wondered why I never saw you in the waiting room again. How did that divorce stuff work out? You're looking better."

Donna smiled thinly. "Things are still rotten, but I started a flower business doing arrangements for weddings only. It's going real well and has given me less time to think about Judd. Dealing only with stressed out brides has its pitfalls, but at least they don't send nasty-grams in the mail three times a week. How about you?"

"Things are good."

Donna noticed that when he smiled his eyes lit up in an appealing way.

"Well, I hate to hit and run, but I need to get this food up to my church."

"Is that the place on 147th that does the Wednesday night dinners?"

"That's us. Best chicken, ham and potatoes in town. And you can't beat the price."

"Maybe I'll check it out sometime. Well, I'll see you. Good luck with the weddings. Hopefully the local flowers will come through." He backed his cart up and went around her.

"Thanks, great to see you." Donna couldn't help but glance into Tony's cart as he passed. One bag of apples, one bag of carrots and a loaf of bread, even though she'd knocked into him at the corner of canned goods and rice. Interesting.

It wasn't until Donna was unloading her car at the church's kitchen door that it struck her…how did Tony know anything about the hydrangea problem? Before she could think anything more about it, the chief cook was yelling for the lettuce.

The next Wednesday, Donna could barely drag herself to the store and on to the church. One of the many much-too-fat letters in the mail from her husband's attorney had left her teary for most of the day. Her own attorney was out of town and she couldn't even get him on his cell phone, so she had spent the afternoon in a dark funk.

Edwinna MacDonald had come to enjoy her friendship with Donna. In their once-a-week, side-by-side positions on the chow line, she admired Donna's easy manner with their guests, her cheerful smile, and the warmth in her voice as she greeted each person. Donna could make "Would you like gravy with that?" sound like a personal invitation to the most expensive restaurant in town.

Tonight, Donna had been late, creating a minor crisis in the kitchen as everyone worked double-time to get the salad thrown together and the rolls tossed into baskets and distributed on the tables. It wasn't until Edwinna took her place behind the counter several minutes before the doors opened that she could see how upset her friend was.

"What is it? What's happened?" she asked with concern, giving the corn in her warming pan a stir.

Donna shook her head. "I can't talk about it. It's this divorce, I can't stand it anymore."

"Do you have a good attorney?"

"Yeah. An old friend from high school. He actually changed careers and got his law degree a couple years ago. He's giving me a really good deal. I think he likes me…he always did in high school."

"But wait. Is he a divorce attorney?"

"I guess."

"There's no *guessing.*" Edwinna was emphatic. "Do you know anyone else he's represented in a divorce?"

"Not really."

"How did you get on to him?"

"He called me up and offered. He'd heard through the alumni grapevine, I guess."

"*Please* tell me you and your husband didn't go to high school together. Tell me this man doesn't know both of you."

"Well, of course he does. We all went to school together."

Incredulous, Edwinna hit the pan so hard with her big aluminum spoon that six corn kernels jumped out. "Donna, don't you see? Your husband has set you up!"

"Don't be silly—"

"I'm giving you the number of my divorce attorney, Judith Cisneros. She's wonderful. I want you to talk with her, then you can decide."

The doors opened and the waiting line spilled into the room in a booming cacophony of voices, color and movement.

Donna stirred the glistening gravy thoughtfully. *It couldn't be possible, could it? No. It wasn't possible.* But throughout the evening, while her hands, voice and smile greeted, offered, consoled, and cooed at toddlers, her brain was reviewing every interaction she'd had with her attorney since the beginning. By the time the last plate had been washed and dried, the tables wiped and put away, and the final crumb sent down the garbage disposal, Donna's head was ready to explode. A new determination burned inside her. She slipped the number of Edwinna's attorney into her purse, convinced that first thing in the morning, the tide was about to turn on her husband.

Donna was rushing. She had accounted for every variable as she prepared for her biggest job yet, flowers for a wedding and reception for 300 at the most popular winery in the county, a beautiful venue that she had visited twice in preparation for this day. Every variable, that is, except for extraordinary heat for a late July wedding. It was going to be nearly 90 degrees, and she was worried that the flowers would wilt in her second-hand van with its sub-par air conditioning system that could only manage "less warm" rather than "cool." *I should have gotten it fixed before this*, she berated herself as she loaded the rest of the flower boxes through the rear doors. But it was only a forty-five minute drive, and she had the timing down to the minute in terms of arrival with the bouquets, corsages and boutonnières for the wedding party, the centerpieces for the tables, and the large vases for the wedding itself. She slammed the temperamental rear doors shut, made one last trip into the garage to grab her briefcase, and was off.

Making good time on the back roads far outside the city, a dog suddenly darted out from the brush beside the road. Donna braked and swerved quickly, missing the dog, but her tires hit some debris. Within a minute she heard the heart-stopping "thump-a-thump-a-thump" of a flattening tire and her steering wheel pulled sharply to the right. She coasted to a stop, disbelief spreading along with a chilling fear from her head to her chest as she jumped out and looked at the right front tire, now completely flat and resting on the rim.

"Shit! Shit! Shit! *Shit!*" She kicked the sorrowful tire in frustration, then went back to her purse and quickly found her AAA card to call for roadside help. Hearing the situation, the operator promised to send the first available truck to help her, but it would still be nearly an hour. Donna rested her head against the driver's door. She would have to call the bride and ask her to send someone, or several someones, to come rescue the flowers before they wilted. It wasn't the end of the world, she consoled herself. Just unbelievable bad luck. Tears welled in her eyes. It had been so important to do a good job on this wedding. The families on both sides were well-connected and most likely could bring her many more contacts. *Oh, well.* She might as well make the call and get it over with.

She rolled through her phone contact list to find the bride's number. Hopefully she would have her cell phone nearby. But before Donna could hit send, a blue van passed slowly beside her, then pulled over and parked in front. Donna paused, then broke into a smile as Tony Wagner descended from the driver's door.

"Tony! What are you doing here?" she exclaimed.

"I'd ask you the same thing. What happened?"

"A dog ran out in front of me, I swerved and must have hit something. I've got a whole load of flowers for a four o'clock wedding, and I can't get any help for an hour. I was just about to call the bride and ask her to send me a couple of cars."

"Well, listen, I've got an empty van here. Why don't we trade cars. I'll wait with yours till the roadside assistance truck gets here, you take mine and get on your way. I'll meet you at your house later and we'll trade back."

"Could you really do that? Are you sure you don't mind? This is such an important wedding for me, the biggest one I've done since starting the business."

"What are we standing here for, let's get the flowers transferred!"

With Tony's help, Donna quickly had the boxes moved into the other van and was on her way.

Too late, she realized she had forgotten to get Tony's phone number. And it was another two hours before the thought entered her mind that he would have no idea where she lived. She figured she'd have to try to find him through Liz somehow. So it was a surprise to arrive home three hours later and find her van, now balanced on four full tires, sitting in the driveway and Tony lounging on her front porch swing reading a book.

"How did you find me?" she smiled happily.

"Your registration was in the glove compartment."

"Was there any trouble with the spare tire?"

"Nope. I stopped and got your tire fixed. And the spare is back in the well. So you're all set to go. Your air conditioning isn't very good, though, I have to tell you. And you probably should get some new tires soon."

"I know, the van's not the greatest, but it's all I can afford right now. You really saved me today." She dropped his van keys into his outstretched hand. "Do you want to come in and have a drink of something cool? And what do I owe you for the tire?"

"The tire's on the house. I've got a friend down at the tire store to whom I give a lot of business. I'd better be on my way. It was nice to see you again."

"What a coincidence, really. The first time I met you we were rescuing Liz, now this time you're rescuing me."

"My pleasure." He gave her a sincere smile and went to his van. "How did the wedding work out?" he called back.

"Stunningly. The flowers looked gorgeous. The bride was radiant and so happy. This was a big day for me."

"Glad I could be a part of it." With that he nodded his head and was off. He glanced in his rear view mirror; Donna was watching him go.

A week later, it had been a long afternoon in the van. Donna had arranged and delivered flowers for two different weddings on opposite sides of the city. Exhausted, she wanted nothing more than a warm bath and to take a short nap before dinner. As she pulled into the driveway, she noted a tendril of smoke exiting her sixteen-year-old son's bedroom window.

"James!" She knocked and opened his door in the same movement. "What are you doing?"

He was standing at the window and dropped the oddly shaped cigarette out when his mother burst in.

"Nothing, Mom."

"You know I don't want you smoking. It's terrible for you."

"I wasn't smoking."

"Of course you were. The only question is *what* were you smoking, and I think it was pot. Where are you getting it?"

"It's no big deal, Mom, honest. I'm not hurting anyone."

"It *is* a big deal! It's still illegal and you're under age anyway. Smoking isn't going to make anything go away for more than twenty minutes."

"It relaxes me, that's all."

"I don't care. Trying cleaning, that's relaxing. Twirl a toilet brush, scrub a sink, do a load of laundry. It's all very relaxing."

"Mom—"

"I mean it. You've just pushed back getting your license by another three months. At this rate you're going to be 96 before you can drive yourself anywhere."

James' voice was raised now. "That's so unfair. Dad'll let me drive, I know. He thinks you're being really mean."

Bringing her husband into it was a low blow.

"We'll discuss this later. I'm taking a nap, I'll see you at dinner." She pulled the door closed harder than she needed to, stomped down the stairs and into the yard beneath his window. The joint lay in the azalea bush where it had fallen. She brought it in and soaked it at the kitchen sink, then threw it in the trash.

Lying on her bed, she tried to remember the happiness she'd felt after delivering the flowers. It was hard sometimes to be in the presence of such unbridled joy around the weddings, when her own marriage was twirling the drain in a wicked and disheartening death spiral. How had she missed the tell-tale signs of Taffy's crush on her husband? She was right there in the store with them every day. The girl was only fifteen years older than their own daughter, for heaven's sake. Just because she was pretty, and thin, and batted her eyes at him. And had beautiful, honey-colored hair. Donna's eyes welled with tears. She hadn't realized Judd's extensive hours at his new hobby of golf had really been spent in the sack with Taffy, whose apartment happened to be right across the street from the driving range. "Hitting a bucket of balls" had certainly taken on a new meaning in this family.

Donna managed a quick 20 minutes of unconsciousness before the banging back door woke her. The girls were arguing. Robyn, seventeen years old, had been tasked with dropping off and picking up her fourteen-year-old sister Violet at the mall.

"You were supposed to be out front at five o'clock," Robyn dropped her purse on the sideboard and hung the car keys up on the hook where they were kept. "I had to wait twenty minutes for you."

"Oh, big deal," Violet retorted. "You weren't doing anything anyway. We were all the way at the other end getting pizza and it took longer than we expected."

"That's why you've got a watch."

"Hello, girls," Donna tried to enter cheerily. "I had a great afternoon. How about you?"

"Robyn and Rick broke up," Violet broke the news joyously, as she hadn't ever cared for her sister's boyfriend of the past six months. He spent way too much time hogging the couch watching sports on the living room television.

"Shut *up*!" Robyn cried, bursting into tears and taking off for her room.

"I'm sorry to hear that," Donna started to say. She waited until Robyn was up the stairs before asking for the details from Violet. Apparently, Rick was about to take off on a European adventure with his parents for the last few weeks of summer, and was looking for some leniency in their exclusivity agreement.

"Ouch," Donna was sympathetic. Rick was Robyn's first real boyfriend. "And listen, Violet, you need to be a little more compassionate, and also appreciative of your sister giving you rides. Without her, you'd be stuck at home a lot more often."

"I wish James would hurry up and get his license. Then I'd have double the chance of getting where I need to go."

"Yeah, well, don't hold your breath on that one."

Dinner was going as well as could be expected with a distraught daughter, an angry son, and an annoyingly cheerful young teen. They were just starting dessert when the children's father called. Robyn took the phone, and was suddenly calling excitedly to the others.

"Dad's got tickets to Hawaii!! For next week! He has a convention and he wants to take us. How cool is that?" The others clambered to the extension phones so they could listen in.

"Hold on," Donna tried to get their attention. "We were going to go over to the islands, just the four of us, like we always do, remember? I've purposely not taken any weddings next weekend so we can go."

"Okay, Dad, that would be great!" Ignoring her mother, Robyn wrapped up the phone call on her end.

"Come in here, all of you," Donna yelled so she could be heard throughout the house.

"What?" James was antagonistic. "So we get to go somewhere different in August for a change. What's the big deal?"

Donna glanced at her daughters, hopeful for some support, but she knew they missed their father, scum that he was. Dangling Hawaii—where they'd always wanted to go, where they had promised many times they would take vacation as a family but they'd never been able to—dangling this in front of these three who were trying to figure out how their world had turned oddly upside down—was more conniving than even Donna could have given him credit for.

"We could go to the San Juans for a long weekend in September, couldn't we?" Violet asked. "I've always wanted to go to Hawaii. And Dad said we're in a hotel with one of those wonderful lagoon pools!"

Donna left the dining room table and started doing the dishes, tears sliding down her cheeks. How low could he go?

By the end of September, Donna had hit bottom. After a wonderful time in Hawaii with their father, who was so loving and attentive and generous and established no discipline whatsoever, the teens arrived home picking fights with their mother and each other. Donna's efforts to get everyone back on track at the start of school were failing. James was smoking more and staying out late. Robyn had a small car accident when she was texting while driving, and Violet had been in trouble at school for skipping P.E. to avoid the mile run two Fridays in a row. Then the three returned from their Tuesday dinner at their father's with a bombshell announcement: He'd invited them to move in with him and Taffy for the school year.

"Can you imagine?" Donna confided in Edwinna behind the serving line on Wednesday evening. "He's promised them everything."

Unnoticed, Tony had come in the social hall doors and waited patiently until Donna looked up from her turkey and gravy pans and saw him leaning against the wall. The sight of his compassionate smile made tears come to her eyes. She asked another volunteer to take over her spot and went over to say hello.

"Thought I'd check this place out," he said. "I go past it almost every day."

"There's still plenty of food if you'd like a plate," Donna indicated the end of the line.

"No, thanks, I already ate. But I'm happy to help if there's something I can do."

Donna introduced him around and liked the way he pitched right in putting the tables away.

"Thanks for helping tonight," Donna said as they carried the empty food crates to her van together. "We were a little short on volunteers."

"Glad to. Is there anything else I can do?"

Donna hesitated. Four hours volunteering had not made her feel much better.

Tony cleared his throat. "I've started taking a short walk each evening. Even in the dark it can be quite peaceful."

"That's funny, I do the same thing. I go to escape the kids sometimes, to be honest about it."

"Would it be too forward to go home with you, then we could walk together?"

Donna was torn. Her instinct was to say no, to go off by herself and be miserable. She knew the conversation with the kids about moving to their dad's would begin the moment she walked through the door. She glanced at Tony, with his kind smile.

"I *could* use a walk tonight. Though what I'd really like is a beer, but I'm off alcohol at the moment. Can you drink and walk at the same time?"

"I'm a cola man myself. And yes, I can drink and walk at the same time. I couldn't always say that, I'm afraid."

Donna led the way to her home, a few miles from the church. Tony parked several houses back and let Donna check on the kids. She reappeared with a root beer for herself and a cola for Tony. A cool breeze brushed them as a waning moon and the first stars appeared in the perfectly cloudless sky.

They chatted about Liz and what was happening in their weeks. Donna told Tony about the kids moving out, and he listened sympathetically.

"What is it that you do, exactly?" Donna finally inquired.

"Consulting."

"What kind of consulting?"

"General consulting."

If ever there was a conversation stopper, that seems to be it, Donna thought curiously.

Tony introduced a new topic, and soon they had completed the circle and were back at her house.

"Thanks for the company," Donna placed her arm lightly on his sleeve.

"Maybe we could do it again sometime. I enjoy being with you."

"Sure, that would be great."

"Could I call you? Just to check in? Since it's such a hard week and all? You know how Liz says we're supposed to reach out to others."

"Yeah, I've heard that a few times myself. Sure, you can call. Let me give you my cell number."

They exchanged numbers. Donna waited in front of her house until Tony had gotten in his car and pulled away. She gave him a little wave. Something about being with Tony inspired confidence and comfort…she just couldn't quite put her finger on what it was.

The next Saturday, Donna had her computer open and was trying to check her list against the array of flowers laid out ready to box up. There was a big wedding at 2:00. The venue was an hour away, and she wanted to have the flowers there by 11:30. The kids were in the house packing up their bags to move to their father's, calling and yelling to each other as they decided what to take and what to leave. James had interrupted her four times already trying to gather all his sport clothes from the laundry corner of the garage. Donna made herself concentrate. It was almost 10:30; she needed to go in and say goodbye to them. Even if they still came over for Tuesday night dinners and every-other weekend, it felt like she was losing them for good. She steeled herself and tried to garner some happy thoughts. They had seen enough of a weepy mother. She would get through this with a smile somehow. Robyn's going didn't bother her so much; by next year she'd be off to college anyway. And James was being such a pill it might be good for him to be around his dad.

But Violet was only 14, still enjoyable, *most* of the time, anyway.

Her plan was a quick walk through the house to say her goodbyes, then packing up the flowers. But when she entered the living room and saw their stack of luggage at the door, she burst into tears.

"Oh, Mom," Robyn came down the stairs with her bed pillow in hand. "It'll be okay. We're only four miles away."

"I'm going to give each of you a hug then be on my way." Donna held out her arms and kissed her daughter on the cheek. "Violet! James! Come say goodbye!"

Violet appeared from the back, gave her mom a good hug, and looked as if she might be rethinking this great adventure. James yelled from upstairs, "I'm on the phone!"

"Well, goodbye!" his mom called up to him. And possibly good riddance, at least for a little while.

"Be good," she said simply, then returned to the garage.

She was boxing arrangements with tears streaming down her face when Tony called.

"How are you doing?" his voice was kind.

"I was fine till I saw all their luggage at the front door. Like they can't wait to get out of here," she sniffled, counting flowers as she spoke.

"It's going to be a tough day. Can I call you tonight?"

"I don't know, Tony. I'm not going to be good company."

"I like your company any way I can get it. I'll call and see what you're doing late afternoon, okay?"

"All right."

"Hey, and listen, you're probably upset and distracted. Be sure you've got all your stuff."

"Yeah, I always do."

"I won't keep you, then. I'll call you later."

Donna arrived at the venue, a beautiful old mansion on the edge of a small river. She had all the flowers laid out in the side room, but something didn't look right. She went through the list again in her head: Bride, groom, parents, grandparents, six bridesmaids, six groomsmen, two extra ushers, one flower girl. Big ceremony piece, table flowers, cake topping flowers, food table flowers, guest book table—Donna's hand flew up to her forehead. Where was the tossing bouquet that would sit at the guest book table? She ran back out to the van and searched, then popped open her computer and looked at her checklist. No "packed it" checkmark beside Tossing Bouquet, which was the last item squeezed onto the bottom of page one. She had missed it when she double-checked. She could remember making it this morning, but what had she done with it? She closed her eyes to concentrate: she had been wrapping the pale blue ribbon tape around the stems when James came out to find his soccer uniform, she'd walked over to the dryer...that's it. She'd put it down on top of the dryer to dig through the clothes there. And then not picked it back up. Well, it was too far to go home for it.

Donna pulled out her emergency box in the van. Her tapes, wraps, scissors, water tubes and a few less than perfect extra flowers filled the container. This was going to be tricky. She grabbed the best of the extra flowers to add some bulk, then went back to the side room and deftly lifted flowers out of the other arrangements and bouquets (leaving the bride's bouquet unscathed) until she had enough blossoms to make a tightly compacted circle in similar colors as the bride's. It was a smidge smaller than normal, but hopefully enough wine would have flowed by the time the bride threw it, no one would notice.

"What's a tossing bouquet?" Tony asked later that afternoon as he heard the story on the phone.

"Today's brides don't want to give away their own bouquet. Especially if they're not flying off on a honeymoon and will be around to enjoy it. So we make a smaller bouquet for them to use for the throwing. It usually sits on the place card table, or guestbook table. It's a good thing there were so many bridesmaids' and table flowers, I could pilfer enough without wrecking anything."

"You are remarkably gifted," Tony complimented her. Sitting comfortably on the couch in his living room, he glanced at his open laptop in front of him. Donna's flower checklist was pulled up, the Tossing Bouquet line with its missing check off mark highlighted. "How about some dinner? Would you like to go out?"

"I'm beat, really."

"What if I invite myself over with some Chinese in hand?"

Donna was cleaning up her work space. She realized she had been avoiding going into the empty house for the past two hours. Maybe it *would* be a good evening to have some company.

"Sure, Chinese sounds great."

The second night after the children left, Donna began upping the vengeance in her Taffy fantasies as she lay in bed at night. She imagined a bouquet filled with beautiful but deadly flowers that would creep up and strangle the woman on her wedding day. Or Taffy's first Thanksgiving with her future mother-in-law sharing the kitchen. It had taken Donna fifteen years to establish a reasonable pattern of movement in the kitchen with Esmeralda so that they weren't bumping into each other the entire day. She imagined Taffy stuffing a twenty-pound bird with Esmeralda peering over her shoulder and trying to get her hand in, or to mix up anything without Esmeralda coming along behind, tasting and adding seasoning. Donna envisioned the holiday dining room, where the little nieces and nephews would be eating and spilling...Oh, so sorry, Aunt Taffy, as a tall glass of cranberry juice upends across the white linen table cloth. And then to the living room: Oopsie! As the top comes off a toddler's sippy cup and the milk spills down the couch cushions. Or as a preschooler scribbles on the pale green carpet with markers, as her mother looks questionably at the dark streaks of color and asks the surrounding adults: Are these the invisible markers you shouldn't be able to see?

Or next spring: While playing golf, Taffy is knocked on the head by an errant golf ball. Doesn't kill her, of course, or hurt her very much. Not really. Her tawny swirl of thick honey-colored bouffant hair saved her. Too bad.

Maybe that lovely hair turns prematurely gray from the stress of three teens going back and forth between houses. Wouldn't that be a terrible sight?

Donna tried to feel some shame, but none came. Instead she rolled onto her back, took some slow deep breaths, and concentrated on a mind clearing exercise she remembered from a yoga class years ago. She felt her muscles relax a bit, and thought it was working. Until one last thought popped into her head—maybe some of Judd's little annoying habits might begin to drive Taffy crazy. Like the way he couldn't get a wet towel on a towel bar. Or a dirty dish in the dishwasher. Or lock the garage door. Or find his keys. Ever. Or…and she was surprised it took so long to think of it…perhaps his snoring, with sounds that made Felix Unger's noises seem like a French mime, would send dear Taffy fleeing to a separate bedroom.

Donna smiled and finally drifted off to sleep.

Four weeks later, the fireplace danced with the light of good hardwood logs being burned, sending shadows flashing around the walls of the living room. Donna checked the small roast and vegetables she had placed in the oven an hour earlier, then carried two wine glasses and a bottle of sparkling apple cider to the coffee table. Over the past month, they had enjoyed several dinners out. They took turns finding places the other had never been. So far they'd eaten at the Space Needle, a Greek restaurant, an Ethiopian cafe, and even tried a vegetarian place nearby. But today, since she hadn't had a wedding delivery, she'd offered to cook for him.

The familiar knock on the front door occurred at precisely 6:30. Tony handed Donna a small, lovely chocolate cake, a departure from the fairly healthy eating they had been observing for the last month.

"What's this?" Donna accepted the dessert with a smile.

"It's our four-month anniversary from the day you had the flat tire."

"You're so silly. Come on in." Hanging his coat on the rack, Donna had the sudden realization that she was—momentarily—happy.

After dinner they moved to the living room. Tony sat down first, placing his left arm along the back of the sofa. Donna arrived with two pieces of cake. Setting them on the coffee table, she sat beside Tony, once again letting the strange feeling of happiness wash over her as she leaned against him a bit and his arm fell lightly around her shoulders.

"Thanks for dinner. It was delicious."

"You're welcome."

The glowing fire sent sparks floating mystically up the chimney with a crackle. Their silence was comfortable. Tony let his hand rest on Donna's shoulder, giving it a small squeeze. Donna moved a little closer into his side.

"You've been a wonderful friend these past few months," Donna said appreciatively. "I don't know how I could have gotten through."

Tony pushed a strand of her dark hair off her face. His finger lingered on her cheek's smooth skin.

"Since the first time I saw you in Liz's waiting room, I've been waiting for an evening like this," he said softly. Donna tilted her head upward and toward his, and he leaned in.

Their lips had barely met when there was stomping on the front stoop and the sound of a key in the lock. Donna jerked away as the door opened and Robyn popped through with James and Violet right behind.

"Mom?" Robyn first looked left at the dining room table set for two, then to the right and discovered her mother on the couch with a strange man. "We're home."

Tony made his exit after being introduced and helping to carry in the kids' luggage. Donna sat at the kitchen table while each child in turn described the end of the great adventure of living with their dad and his mistress.

"She doesn't know how to cook at all," Robyn started. "There was never any food in the house. Every evening it was a three-hour ordeal to get dinner on the table."

Donna felt bad about that. Judd actually knew his way around the kitchen; cooking was one of the things they used to enjoy doing together.

"And laundry," James intoned. "She shrank all my uniforms the very first wash. I tried to be a good sport, but geez. My shorts are up to my crotch now."

"I don't suppose you might have offered to do your own laundry?"

"No way. She's so fussy. She didn't want us touching anything."

"And she wouldn't share her car," Robyn concluded. "Mine had to be in the shop, and I had to get up to school for play practice, and she wouldn't let me take hers. And she didn't want to give me a ride, either, said it would make her late for work. I had to call fifteen people to find someone who could pick me up."

"Hmm." Make no comments, Donna told herself. Show no emotion. Let them vent.

"It wasn't really that bad," Violet finally had her say. "But I missed you. Dad's head is up his ass...he was crazy to leave you for her."

"Violet! Your language!" Donna was appalled.

"Taffy talks like that all the time," James said. "Violet's picked up some new vocabulary beyond what she's learning at middle school."

Donna brought them more milk to wash down the chocolate cake. As she glanced at her children, seated in their regular places at the breakfast table, trying to outdo each other with their stories of Taffy's failings, the rough-edged rip right down the center of her tender, aching heart began to heal just a little.

Chapter Four: Chrissy

June—November, 2011

"I don't think I'm passive-aggressive," the young woman said quietly to her therapist as she calmly snapped the head off the anatomically incorrect Barbie doll in her hands.

"Really?" Dr. Mark Fleming held out his palm to receive the doll pieces. He replaced Barbie's head, then returned her to his tub of toys for young patients. He studied the slender girl before him. "You seem to have some pretty strong feelings about things, but not many positive ways of letting them out."

"I've said I'm sorry about lying to my parents. I don't know why Liz had to switch me to you."

"She was under some ethical constraints, you know. She couldn't act as if she'd counseled you and received money from your parents when she hadn't…when you sat in the waiting room instead and pocketed the payment."

"I only did that a few times. Less than six."

"But Liz was thankful you helped out when she was ill. With finding the dog and all. So the compromise of not telling your parents was to switch you to me. With direct payment to prevent a—relapse, shall we say?"

Chrissy uncrossed her long legs, then recrossed them. She reached into the toy bin and pulled out a tennis ball, tossing it back and forth between her hands. He was nice enough, this partner of Liz's. Seemed kind. Probably trustworthy.

"Do you have kids of your own?" she finally asked him.

"I do."

"Any teenagers?"

"Not quite yet. The oldest is nine."

"I bet when they're eighteen you're going to let them out of the house. To live, I mean. To go off to college or something."

"You've been to college, haven't you? You're twenty-two."

"But I lived at home." The tennis ball was tossed rather recklessly into the bin. The lanky young woman reached in and pulled out an old green Gumby, folding his arms and legs into a tight sphere.

"Gumby's taking a fetal position, I see," Dr. Fleming commented dryly.

Chrissy tossed Gumby back into the bin, jumped to her feet, and went to the window. She couldn't stand it, not for one more minute. Her head was going to burst if she didn't tell someone.

"I've messed up big time," she said quietly, looking beyond the buildings out to the horizon. A few blue streaks of clear sky showed through the low clouds. How she would like to be on a plane, soaring above it all, flying away, far away, with the earth becoming smaller and smaller beneath.

Dr. Fleming waited patiently. He and Liz had traded patients a few times for various reasons, but this client was especially dear to Liz. It had pained her to have to switch. He felt compelled to attempt some headway with what, at first, appeared to be a selfish, narcissistic young woman with parent problems. But after only a few sessions the complexity of Chrissy's personality had been showing forth as she alternately destroyed his toys or inexplicably agreed with everything he said.

"Last month I told my parents I'm pregnant," Chrissy said to the window.

"I'm sorry?" Mark wasn't sure he had heard correctly.

Chrissy strolled with pointed defiance back to her upholstered chair, sinking into it, finally making eye contact for the first time.

"I told my parents I'm pregnant." She dropped her eyes as quickly as she had focused them on him.

"Are you?"

"No. I thought they'd be furious. I thought they'd throw me out of the house. I thought they'd disown me. They've been talking about nothing except graduate school all year. A pregnancy would ruin all their plans."

"So what happened?"

"They were shocked, of course. They've never even met Kevin. I tried to make him sound awful, like I was only one in a long string of girlfriends."

"But?"

"They're thrilled. It only took twenty-four hours for them to adjust to it. Now they're worse than ever. I should be careful of everything, because I'm pregnant. They still think I have an eating disorder, so they're on me all the time about what I eat. Now I should eat more; I'm eating for two. I should eat better; I'm eating for two. I should sleep more, and rest more, and be more careful. I can't drink or smoke."

"*Do* you smoke?" Mark had never noticed any odor on her clothing.

"No, only around them to annoy them. That was another ploy to try to get thrown out. I started when I was sixteen."

"Chrissy, these deceptions—"

"My mother's buying baby clothes...." Her head went into her hands, and she crumpled visibly, heaving with great wracking sobs that seemed too large to come from her slim body. "What am I going to do?"

He nudged the tissue box on the floor closer to her with his foot, but didn't interrupt her crying. When she had quieted, he asked gently, "What was your original plan?"

She took a tissue and blew her nose, wiping her eyes, but tears still streamed down her cheeks.

"I was going to move in with Kevin, and then, in a couple months, tell them I miscarried. They'd be used to having me out of the house, and maybe it would all be okay."

Mark went to his desk, picked up the top file and flipped through the first pages.

"Remind me. I'm sorry I can't seem to find it. Why are your parents so unreasonably controlling?"

Chrissy sighed and wiped her eyes again.

"My mother had two babies before me who died in the last month of her pregnancies. When she carried me to full term, and I was okay, they quit trying for any others. I've been the vessel for all their hopes and dreams for twenty-two years. *I'm* not the one who should be in therapy. They're good people, really, but...I've never been able to live. Really live. When Liz went missing in May, we had just gotten to the point where we were going to have a showdown with them. She was going to help me try to break away. But then I got cold feet."

"What would you like to do…if you were financially independent and could do anything? What was your goal in college?" Mark settled back into his chair, newly sympathetic to his client's predicament and trying to plan the best way to support her.

"I wanted to go to medical school."

"Really?" That hadn't been the answer he expected. Fashion or marketing seemed more fitting for her skinny girl profile.

"I took the MCAT. I applied to twenty schools." Her head dropped and tears started flowing again.

"You never told your parents? They didn't even notice you studying, or the applications in the mail? The fees? None of it?"

"No. I used Kevin's address. And so much is online now. They have no idea."

"So that's a disappointment for you; your plans aren't working out."

"I got into ten." Her voice dropped the way it always did when she wanted to become invisible.

"I'm sorry? I couldn't hear you." He waited patiently for whatever it was she was having trouble expressing.

She held up her head and made eye contact again.

"I got into ten schools. I'm going to the University of Washington."

"You got in? You got in *ten*? That's incredible, isn't it? I thought these last three years had some of the toughest competition for med school. Kids are ecstatic to get in just one, and you got in ten?"

She nodded.

"Wouldn't your parents be so proud of you? Wouldn't they be so happy to have a daughter who's a doctor?"

"I'd have to live at home." Tears rolled down her cheeks again. "They'll never let me go."

Three weeks later, Chrissy entered the waiting room, her mother and father following through the door. Mrs. Thomas took in the neutral-toned fabric on the comfortable chairs and couch, the calming photographs attractively displayed, and the contrasting blue on the far wall, exuding happiness. Her thoughts flashed ahead to decorating the nursery, but she instantly pulled herself back from that. Too soon, she knew. She would hold her excitement in check until the last possible moment. Too many bad things could happen.

Mr. Thomas took a seat and picked up the sports magazine lying on the end table. He had left work early to make this appointment. His wife had been insistent that they attend since the new counselor had specifically called and invited them. He glanced at Chrissy, perched in the straight backed chair by the door. He wasn't yet used to the idea of her being a mother, she was much too young. And should anything go wrong…well, he couldn't go through that again.

"Mr. and Mrs. Thomas?" Dr. Fleming came around the corner. "Hello, Chrissy. Come on back."

He led the way to his office, where he had strategically stationed the chairs so that Chrissy would sit beside him, across from her parents. Mrs. Thomas took the chair by the window with her husband next to her. It felt a little odd to be in a counseling office, but she was willing to do anything for Chrissy's health.

Once they were all settled, Dr. Fleming addressed Chrissy's parents calmly and directly, making good eye contact.

"Thank you for coming today. As you know, I've been seeing Chrissy for about a month, and I wanted to check in with you on her progress."

Chrissy was alternately sitting on her hands or pulling her long sleeves down over her fingers, crossing her legs first one way and then the other, clearly uncomfortable.

"First, I have some good news to report." Chrissy's stomach flip-flopped, and she could barely concentrate on what Dr. Fleming was saying. "Chrissy no longer appears to have an eating disorder. She has a normal, healthy appetite and is making good food choices."

"I knew it," Mrs. Thomas beamed. "It's because of the baby, I know it is."

"Yes, well, that's the next thing. Chrissy, would you like to talk to your parents about that?"

Chrissy wanted to bolt for the door. She actually measured the distance and wondered if she could get there before they reached out to stop her. Real nausea, not the fake stuff she'd been pretending to have for weeks, was rising up her esophagus. She stared at the intricate design in the carpet and tried to remember the words she and Dr. Fleming had rehearsed and practiced.

"Mom and Dad," her voice wavered and she couldn't go on.

"What is it, honey?" her mom asked cheerily, somehow missing all the visual signals in front of her. Mr. Thomas' face changed from benign interest to concern as he registered Chrissy's distress.

"Mom and Dad," Chrissy tried again. "I have been dishonest with you. Terribly dishonest." Her eyes were still glued to the floor. "I do have a boyfriend named Kevin. A wonderful, wonderful guy. But I'm not pregnant. I never was. I just said that because I thought you'd throw me out and then I could go live with him." Tears started down her cheeks, and she raised her head enough to glance at her mother.

"I don't understand," Mrs. Thomas' head tilted questioningly. "What do you mean, you're not pregnant?"

"I never was pregnant. I just said that. I wanted to move out, I want to be with Kevin. I thought you'd be so angry that you'd throw me out of the house. It was stupid, I know, and hurtful. But you reacted differently than I expected."

There was a great chasm of painful silence in the room. Dr. Fleming watched both parents look at their daughter and gauged their reactions. He wasn't sure if Mr. Thomas didn't seem a bit relieved.

"I know this must be difficult," he started softly.

"I don't understand," Mrs. Thomas said again, this time more loudly. "I mean, why would you say such a thing? How could you? After…after…after everything that's happened?"

"Mom, I know. I'm sorry. I'm so sorry, it was stupid. I wasn't thinking. I just got the thought in my head and then blurted it out and then I couldn't take it back."

"But—" a great gulp of tears exploded from Mrs. Thomas, and Mr. Thomas' arms went around her. She wept into his shoulder. Chrissy looked mournfully at floor, her tears making wet splotches on her black pants.

Mark waited quietly until Mrs. Thomas' tears had subsided a bit.

"May I ask you, if you don't mind, about your losses before Chrissy was born? I'm sure it's difficult to talk about. What a terrible thing to have two pregnancies end in such tragedy."

"The first was a girl." Mrs. Thomas straightened and spoke with poignant resignation. "She was stillborn, they never could tell us what happened. The second was a boy. One day in the ninth month, I didn't feel any movement. Of course I panicked and went right to the ER, but there wasn't anything they could do. It was terrible."

"I'm so sorry. How far apart were the births?"

"About 18 months."

"And then how long until Chrissy was born?"

"Two years."

"And you still think about those children?"

"Of course. They'd be 24 and almost 26 now."

"I see." Mark was quiet again.

Finally, Mrs. Thomas spoke. "I know we were too protective with Chrissy. I know we hovered, and helicoptered, and whatever else they call it now. But you have to understand, I couldn't lose another child."

"I do understand."

"And it hasn't been awful, has it honey? You know how much we love you…." Her voice trailed off.

"I know, Mom," Chrissy said miserably.

"What has happened here," Mark began slowly, "and it's very common in these situations when there has been the loss of a child in a family, is that the dynamic becomes skewed as all the parental expectations land on the surviving child. A family that should have had three children has only one, and that's a big burden for the remaining child. Normal parental concern gets exaggerated, and then normal teen rebellion is inflated against that pressure. Sometimes the remaining child carries some unintended survival guilt that makes it hard to push back against the parents, even in the most normal teenage ways. In Chrissy's case, she could not develop any positive ways to work it out, so she fell into deception to carve herself some space. I'm sure she never meant to hurt you so deeply with this."

Chrissy looked hopefully at her mother, who opened her arms and Chrissy flew across the rug into her embrace, collapsing onto her knees and sobbing once again.

"What are your thoughts, Mr. Thomas?" Mark inquired.

"Quite honestly, I'm relieved." Mr. Thomas wiped his forehead with his hand. "I thought she was too young to have a baby, especially since we don't know the father and they're not married. I had hoped she'd go on to graduate school, though we've had no luck in interesting her in that direction. She'd be so good at business. I thought maybe an MBA. She's really smart. Exceptionally so, we've been told by educational psychologists."

"Well, there is one other piece of good news besides the improvement in her eating habits. Would you like to tell them, Chrissy?"

Chrissy retreated from her mother's arms and sat on her knees, pulling her tear-dampened hair away from her face.

"This will surprise you. But I applied to medical school for next year. And I got in. I'm starting at U.W. in September."

"Medical school!" Her father's voice registered his surprise.

"My daughter, a doctor?" Mrs. Thomas said it slowly, rolling the phrase off her tongue in a pleased way. "Why didn't you tell us?"

"I don't know. I wasn't sure I could get in. I wanted to do something without any help from you." She shot a glance at her father. "I didn't want you to have high expectations and then be disappointed. Honestly, I just wanted something that was all mine."

"I'm so proud of you," her mother managed.

"Me, too," her father concurred, a smile beginning at the corners of his mouth.

"Maybe," Chrissy covered her mother's hands with her own, "maybe someday I can find out why your babies died."

The next day, Mark listened to his messages, the usual calls checking times or asking for reschedules. The last one had come moments before, just as he had been ending a session. Since the message had been nearly incoherent, he dialed back immediately.

"Mrs. Thomas? It's Dr. Fleming."

"Oh…oh. I didn't expect you to call back so quickly. I was wondering. I mean. I thought, I don't know…." Her voice was quavering and tight, as though she had been crying. She started again. "I don't know what to do."

"Yesterday's meeting must have been very difficult for you. I'd like to talk more about that," Mark began compassionately. "Would you like to come in and have some time to work through it together?"

"Do you think...would that be all right? I mean...it's...I'm feeling so strange."

"Strange?"

"Kind of...awful...I don't know. All churned up. It started last night, and I can't seem to get settled down."

Mark consulted his calendar. "I have a cancellation at four today. How would that be? Could you make it then?"

"Yes. I think so. It's so silly, I don't understand."

"You had a big shock yesterday. Your daughter is not quite who you thought she was. It's going to take some time to sort it all out. And the loss of the pregnancy, that's going to stir up a lot of buried feelings. I think you'll find it helpful to have a safe place to talk about all of that."

"I...yes. Yes, I think so. Thank you." Dee Thomas carefully set the receiver in its cradle, then put her head in her hands and wept.

By August, after nearly a month of thrice-weekly sessions with the entire family, as well as private sessions with Mrs. Thomas, Dr. Fleming had most of the kinks worked out of the family's intricate and various interdependent relationships. By the fourth week, more normal interactions between the young adult and her parents were appearing, and Mrs. Thomas seemed to be recovering from her sudden flashbacks and unresolved emotions surrounding her lost pregnancies. Dr. Fleming said he wanted the family to stretch their improved communication skills. After listening to his reasoning, Chrissy and her parents agreed to try his new ideas, designed to break them out of their insular routines. They would drop to one counseling session a week, and together they'd find a place to volunteer to give back to the community, then do one nature-oriented activity each weekend.

The following Wednesday, Mr. Thomas held open the heavy church door for his wife and daughter as they began their first night of helping at the community dinner. At first a mere trickle, an unexpected rush of sorrowful feelings had poured forth in the month of intense counseling sessions with Dr. Fleming. After some reticence, he had been able to express how he had always felt the babies' deaths had affected his wife more deeply, while he remained the steady, supportive one. It was difficult to admit in front of Dee that he hadn't really bonded with the first baby during the pregnancy, being so young and knowing so little about having children. With the second pregnancy, he was too fearful to become attached. But after Chrissy was born, so healthy and perfect, he acknowledged occasional twinges of sadness that there would only be one child to hold and love. Now he had even more compassion for his wife. How terrible for Dee to have carried the babies all those months and then lose them at the end.

In the church's social hall, Marge, the supervisor, sent Mr. Thomas to help set up tables, Mrs. Thomas to put out paper placemats, and brought Chrissy to the kitchen to help finish the salad.

Over the next two hours, Mr. Thomas refilled coffee, Chrissy served up warm brownies with a scoop of ice cream at the dessert station, and Dee Thomas carried a basket of rolls to those seated. Coming behind the kitchen counter for the last of the warm breads, Dee approached the woman who was washing a warming tray in the sink.

"There are so many young families," Dee said softly, under her breath.

"It's not what you expected, is it?" the woman agreed, squirting soap in the pan. "I'm Edwinna," she said with a warm smile. "Thanks for helping out tonight."

"I'm Dee. It's our first time."

Edwinna paused and wiped her hands on her apron, addressing Dee quietly.

"I teach middle school, and the first time I came and saw three of my students coming through the line, I was shocked. You don't expect you could serve 150 people in the suburbs every week."

"What about that table over there with the little kids?" Dee indicated a long table in the far corner of the room where several mothers with toddlers were seated.

"The young mom's table. Well, that first one's husband lost his job, and they're living with his parents. Beside her is Bernadette, that's a really sad case. Her husband became suddenly ill with a progressive neurological condition about four months ago. Then his mom's dementia got worse. They sold their house so they could move in with his mother. They've got that cute little girl Cynthia and another baby due in November. Her husband can take care of himself during the day, but they couldn't afford care for his mother and the little girl, too. So she had to give up her job to stay home. They'll have insurance for about another year, but she's worried. And the third mom's husband is overseas in the military. She's living with her parents who are both on disability."

All the next week, Dee Thomas thought about the table of young mothers. Illness, job loss, and no childcare seemed to be common themes bringing families to the financial edge.

She couldn't do anything about illness and job loss. But childcare, well, she would have to think about that some more.

An early November rainstorm beat against the windows as Dee Thomas observed from the doorway of the infant nursery at the newly opened Grandma's Daycare, established in the childcare room of the church. Next door, the toddler room rocked with joyful shrieks from the one-to-three-year-olds as they measured, dipped, poured, and splashed at the brand new water table.

In one of those inexplicable coincidences that some in the congregation attributed to Divine Intervention, the church had received a generous donation allowing expansion of their community support programs. This had come about right after Dee mentioned her idea of a daycare to Marge and other volunteers at the community dinner. The church council had been thrilled with Dee's proposal to provide childcare for young parents in need. By enlisting several others who were also grandmas-in-waiting, Dee's idea kept costs down by hiring only two paid providers and using volunteers to fill the additional staffing positions.

Dee entered the infant care room, washed her hands, and picked up ten-month-old Gabrielle who had just awakened, crying. Dee settled into the wooden rocker, held the warm body close, and softly sang a nursery rhyme with the baby's head heavy against her shoulder. Tears slowing, Gabrielle's fingers found Dee's shirt and held it tightly in her fist while her eyes studied the room. Dee patted and sang, and soon the baby's head came up and they looked eye-to-eye.

"Ba!" Gabrielle said insistently, pointing a finger.

"Ball?" Dee repeated.

"Ba!" the infant twisted and squirmed, pointing again.

"Sure, we can play ball."

Sliding her to the floor, Dee held out a soft round ball from nearby. The baby took the ball in both hands and moved it up and down, before finally letting go and watching it roll a short distance, laughing with glee. Dee tenderly smoothed the soft blond curls along the angles of Gabrielle's head and handed her the ball again.

Two-thirds of the way through the first quarter of med school, Chrissy was in Biochemistry class in a small, windowless auditorium when the lights blinked once, then extinguished. Emergency generators kicked in and lit the hallways, and a dull glow filled the room as students pulled out their cell phones. As expected, within minutes, an emergency text broadcast arrived from campus security. The entire building had inexplicably gone dark, and classes were being cancelled.

Chrissy exited into the windy, but dry, autumn day and decided to call her mother. Since moving into the graduate student housing at the beginning of the quarter, she'd spent almost no time at home, but still called twice a week or more.

"Hey, Mom!"

"Hi, Chrissy. What's up?"

"Power outage, all the rest of my classes are cancelled today. Do you want to do something? Get lunch?"

"Honey, I'd love to, but I'm out with the girls—Bernie and Cynthia. We're eating and then I'm going to take them to get some clothes and things for the new baby. The doctor told her it could be anytime these next couple of weeks."

An odd feeling came over Chrissy. She could not remember a time when her mother had not jumped at the chance to do something with her.

"Would you like to meet us?"

"No, that's okay. You guys have a good time. Give Bernie a hug for me. I'll call you on the weekend."

Still feeling a little off, Chrissy soaked up the cool sunshine for a moment, finally recognizing that she had absolutely nothing that required her immediate attention.

A group of classmates pushed past, their animated conversation carrying to Chrissy in the breeze; the girl who sat beside her in Biochem turned back.

"We're going for lunch before we do an extra study session for Anatomy," she called. "Want to come?"

"Sure!"

Exhilaration filled Chrissy: the challenge of medical school, the freedom of living on her own, new friends, an open and honest (almost) relationship with her parents, and, best of all, Friday nights spent with Kevin.

She was out of the nest, at last.

Chapter Five: Tony

October—November, 2011

After months of surreptitious surveillance, including but not limited to wiretapping, car following, patient waiting, and occasional just plain good luck, Tony had finally made inroads with Donna, with whom he had become inexplicably smitten in Liz's waiting room the previous May. Now, at the end of October, Liz sat across from him with a frown on her face and her foot tapping a staccato rhythm on the rug as she impatiently waited for him to reply.

Tony was a large man, overweight, nondescript in every way. With his slightly balding head of graying hair, wire rim glasses often pushed up on his forehead, and quiet demeanor, few people noticed that he always sat facing the door, that the watch peeking out under his shirt cuff was one of those military types which practically told the history of the earth as well as the time in seventeen different countries, and that he never went anywhere without his slim briefcase in which his even slimmer and extremely expensive laptop was nestled.

"Nothing's going on," Tony finally answered, gazing calmly at Liz.

"Really? Well, here's what I've heard this month. Donna's church, which was in the red due to their extensive expenditures in programming for the between-the-cracks families and the newly poor, received an extremely generous, anonymous, one-time donation that has put them in the financially healthy column for the first time in fifteen years. They've got enough to start a new daycare program *and* pay off their mortgage if they can manage one fund raiser to get the last ten percent."

"That's wonderful news. I've been to a few of those Wednesday night dinners with Donna. Do you know they feed almost 150 people? All ages? Amazing."

"And, speaking of Donna, that's another interesting thing," Liz's voice was stern. "After months of torturous wrangling, her divorce has been expedited—like water through a sieve. A big settlement is coming her way, she said. Out of the blue, she said, her husband changed his mind and is being cooperative and unbelievably generous. *Out...of...the...blue.*"

"She told me that, too. I'm so happy for her. I think the new attorney has something to do with it."

"Oh, no. She distinctly told me the new attorney, while extremely helpful and much better than her first one, was equally surprised at how quickly things had been resolved...with nearly no explanation. Suddenly a lot of money is coming her way. And the ex is paying *her* attorney's fees. Isn't that odd?"

Tony sat placidly, continuing to meet Liz's steely stare with complete serenity.

"I think it's great. Now she can get on with things."

"You can't do this, Tony. You can't buy your way into her life."

"Who says I had anything to do with it?"

"She's going to find out someday. You can't have secrets this big. It's going to backfire and ruin any chance you have at a real relationship."

"You seem to be assuming something without proof. I had nothing to do with either event."

Liz sighed. It had been August before she'd realized that what Donna had related as good fortune—running into Tony when she needed help with the van's flat tire—hadn't been luck at all, but meticulous planning on his part. She had warned him repeatedly: stalking-like behavior would not be considered normal dating etiquette by a woman in the midst of a bad divorce. Having seen Tony weekly for over ten years, Liz knew him as a kind, thoughtful, extremely bright man with a conflicted past and some paranoid tendencies. She recognized he had fallen in love with Donna, but worried his damaged social skills after two failed marriages might interfere in a normal dating relationship. She had tried to convince him to give Donna some space until her divorce settled. Apparently, he had taken her suggestion more literally than she intended by somehow bringing the case to a quick conclusion. How he had managed that, Liz didn't even want to know.

"I'm enjoying going to church," Tony offered solicitously.

“I’m sure you are.” Liz didn’t mean it to come out quite so sarcastically. “Before you met Donna, how long had it been since you’d darkened the church doors, much less enjoyed it?”

Tony shrugged. “Maybe twenty years or so.”

“So just like that, now you’ve got religion?”

“Are you complaining that I’m feeling the power of a higher authority once again?”

“The only higher authority you believe in is the next generation of electronic gadgets.”

“I take offense at that.” Tony tried to sound wounded.

“Why don’t you open your briefcase and show me what’s new?”

Tony smiled. She knew him too well. He’d try another tack. “I’m helping at the church dinner every Wednesday night. It feels good to do something positive for others who are having a tough time with the economy.”

Liz closed her eyes for a moment and rubbed her forehead. Could she be wrong? Was there any way this relationship was not going to turn into a disaster and leave both her clients with broken hearts? And all because they had run into each other in the waiting room back in May when she had been taken ill. Maybe it was fate after all. Still, she’d never had two clients begin a relationship before, and some ethical considerations made her concerned and cautious.

"How are your parents doing?" she scrolled back into their normal weekly territory: guilt, ill parents far away, the inequities of modern medical care, and sibling relationships or lack thereof.

"I'm going back next week to see them."

A light shone through the detailed glasswork of the living room window as Tony approached his parents' house. Nestled squarely in the middle of an old, North End Boston neighborhood, the home had been the first one built on the block. The modest two-bedroom had been remodeled to expand the living space for a growing family. Traversing the walk from the driveway to the front door flooded Tony with the same memories each visit: his vibrant mother waiting for her raucous crew in the kitchen after school, his father arriving home later with stories of office intrigue and stock market peaks and valleys.

Amelia, the evening caregiver, heard his key in the lock and met him in the hallway.

"Good evening, Mr. Wagner. How was your flight?" Her Dominican lilt filled the quiet house with a heartening welcome.

"Fine, Amelia, thank you. Mom and Dad still awake?"

"Mr. Wagner has retired. Your mother is waiting for you in the library."

The warmth of the cheery room reached out into the cool dimness of the hall. His mother sat facing the fire in her favorite chair. Was it possible for her to shrink in size any further? Soon she would disappear.

"Hi, Mom."

"Antonio!" The petite figure turned at his voice. "I thought you'd be here this afternoon."

"It takes all day to fly what with the time change and all. How are you?" He bent and kissed her wrinkled cheek. "How's Dad?"

"No worse, either of us." She scrutinized him up and down. "Are you losing weight?"

"A little. I'm eating better."

"Because of that woman you were telling me about?" Mrs. Wagner's voice revealed sudden interest in this subject.

"Maybe. We've been trying to exercise, too."

"Well, it's late. Now that you're here, I'm ready for bed. What would you like to do tomorrow?"

"Anything you want. I'm here till Wednesday at two."

"Maybe we could get tickets to the symphony. Or a play. It's been so long since I've been out." Her voice was uncomplaining, but Tony knew she missed the activities she had once enjoyed with his father.

"Of course. Anything you want. I'll look into it in the morning."

The same pretense would be played out each evening, as they decided on an event to attend the next day. But when morning came, invariably Mrs. Wagner did not feel like going out. It would be too cold, too hot, too far, too much walking, or too many people. She would be tired, or a new ache would have surfaced in her legs overnight that was making it difficult to move. Some days her eyes bothered her, some days the ringing in her ears was a nuisance. But regardless, every evening she wanted to make plans.

As his mother inched to the front edge of her chair, Tony pulled the walker close and supported her elbow. She gingerly rose to her feet, then slowly made her way to the new master bedroom that had been created on the first floor. Tony peeked in to see his father sleeping on his side, so small in the bed it was easy to miss him. Pill bottles stood like sentinels on the night stand, while the light from his mother's dressing table cast long shadows around the room. Amelia materialized quietly to help his mother undress.

"See you in the morning, Mom," he kissed her cheek as she passed. "Goodnight, Amelia."

Tony thought again how fortunate the family had been to find good in-home care. Several years ago his sisters had made an effort toward moving his parents to an assisted living facility, but it had become obvious after several frustrating weeks of searching for the perfect fit, his parents were committed to spending the remainder of their lives in the only home they'd known.

The stairway was a testament in pictures to a large family raised with love, organized not chronologically (where he would have been fourth of eight children) but by theme. First were the pictures of the four brothers in their service uniforms. Only he had stayed to become career military, the others had served their duty tours and then mustered out. Next were the four sisters' college graduation pictures, followed by a whole section of wedding portraits. His own two brides still held prominent spots on the wall. His mother often joked she loved both women more than she loved him. At the top of the stairs and continuing down the hall were the pictures of grandchildren, sixteen in all (none of them his), and one new picture at the end of the first great-grandchild.

Entering the third door on the right, the room he had shared with his younger brother throughout high school, he threw his luggage on one twin bed and pulled the cover down on the other. Tiredness overwhelmed him. These trips were necessary, but not without some peril. Both ex-wives lived in Boston; his military service had ended here, somewhat badly; and the accident that had cost him his best friend and nearly his life had happened a mile from this house. His heart began to race even thinking about it. Fifteen years of therapy were only beginning to ease the trauma of two bad years. Two horrendously bad years.

Well, he wouldn't think about it tonight. First placing his phone on the white lace doily beneath the clock and lamp on the bed stand, he changed his mind and decided to call Donna, even though she was most likely making dinner. He sat on the side of the bed and kicked off his shoes while he waited for her to pick up. Her voice seemed cheerful when she answered. He was honored that in August she had ascribed him a special ring tone to discern his calls from the then intimidating ones from her husband and his attorney.

"How are your folks?" she wanted to know first thing. He loved her genuine interest in him and his family. He pushed his glasses onto his forehead, swung his stocking feet up on the bed, and settled back against the pillows. Donna's voice, constant and warm, relaxed him here the same way it did each night at home.

As expected, the next morning his mother did not feel well enough to accompany him to do errands, so he set off alone. In past years, "B.D." (Before Donna), he often hoped to run into either of his ex-wives on these sojourns to the mall. He had parted amicably enough from both, and he felt they retained some feelings for him, although perhaps only the sad fondness one has for an alcoholic uncle who has finally achieved sobriety, if perhaps a tad too late. Both women had remarried honorable men and had children. And both remained in contact with his mother and each other, for reasons he could not fathom. At any rate, now that his relationship with Donna was in bloom, he no longer harbored idiotic reconciliation fantasies or mired himself despondently in old memories and "what ifs."

Unexpectedly running into his ex-wives and having civil discourse was one thing; driving through the intersection of his accident was another. For ten years he had driven four blocks out of his way to avoid that corner. But Liz had told him he should carefully approach this greatest fear each time he was back in Boston, pushing himself a little into discomforting feelings before retreating to safer ground. Supposedly his anxiety would slowly diminish as he repeatedly experienced the intersection in safety. Immediately after the accident, he had not remembered much about that night seventeen years ago, just waking up in the hospital. But with time, and information supplied by others, the evening had recreated itself in fervent Technicolor in both his dreams and unexpected flashbacks.

He had promised Liz he would ease past the intersection as often as possible this trip, coming ever closer to what had become ground zero in his life.

It wasn't the worst flight he'd ever been on, but Wednesday's journey back to Seattle was in the top ten. Terrible turbulence jostled the plane from Montana westward. As they broke through the clouds just before landing, Tony was momentarily disoriented by the large swatches of blackness where the north end of the city should have been.

The flight attendant sitting in the jump seat across from him noticed his concerned stare out the window.

"It's the storm," she yelled over the engine noise. "Huge power outages. We're the last plane in tonight. They're sending some to Portland and holding the rest."

After a rocky, hard set down, Tony rushed to the terminal. He got a weather update from his phone, did a second take at the alarming radar on the small screen, then tried Donna's cell phone as he raced to his car.

She answered on the first ring.

"Tony. I'm so glad you got in safely. I was worried."

"Where are you? Are you at the church?"

"We've got about a hundred people here in the dark. The power blew as we were starting to serve. So we're waiting it out. The wind is terrible; we're all afraid to leave."

"Are your kids okay?"

"They're fine, all home listening to our emergency radio. The blackout is pretty widespread, they said."

"Donna, listen to me carefully. There are huge winds headed your direction, right now, through the north end of the city. Get everyone away from the windows into interior space if you can." He tried desperately to remember how many trees lined the side of the church, hoping they wouldn't come down.

"How do you know?"

"Just believe me, Donna, get people away—"

A thunderous crash, a sharp cry, and Donna was no longer on the phone. Tony, usually unflappable, felt a sickening lurch in his stomach. He redialed Donna's number as he approached his car, but he was transferred right to voice mail.

The rain streamed horizontally, with so much water on the nearly deserted road that hydroplaning was a serious hazard. Neighborhood lights were still on until he entered the north end, when only blackness lay outside his headlight beams. He stayed on the freeway despite the darkness. If he could make it to his exit, he'd only have to go three more blocks to reach one of the numerous garages he had rented throughout the city for his various vehicles, most conveniently located near the freeway.

As his headlights flashed across the stop sign at the top of the exit ramp rise, the view beyond was nearly unrecognizable, trees down everywhere. Two blocks later he had to pull over. Jacket clutched tightly, he made a dash for the garage down the next street, home to his disaster gear and the best emergency vehicle money could buy: a full-size Hummer. Entering by the side door, he used his flashlight to locate the emergency pull on the electric door opener overhead. Three duffel bags and a chain saw were thrown into the back truck compartment first, followed by the rest of his readiness equipment and spare gas.

What Tony couldn't drive over, he drove around; a few fence posts that weren't already flattened took direct hits as he made his way along the street, and sometimes sidewalks, littered with debris. In twenty minutes he was at the church. In the circle of his headlights, all the trees from the southwest side of the church lay toppled, like gigantic toothpicks arranged on the ground.

Pulling the heavy rear Hummer door open against the still fierce gusts, he powered up the chain saw. His headlamp illuminated the main kitchen entrance, where it seemed only limbs, not the entire tree trunk, kept it inaccessible. Making short work of them, Tony then went back for the duffels.

The first person to appear in his lamp light was an ashen-faced Edwinna, who met him in the dark entry, barely lit by the Exit sign glow.

"Tony! Thank God! Do you have others with you?"

"No, it's just me. Where's Donna?"

"She's—it was awful, the wind roaring, the trees coming through the roof. No one had time to move—" Edwinna fought back tears as the terror of the moment returned.

"Where is she?" Tony asked again, more firmly.

Edwinna took a deep breath.

"She's caught under a big limb. She's breathing okay now, not bleeding except a little on her head. She and Ray, tonight's cook, are the worst off, they're the only two we haven't been able to free."

"Show me. Here—" he handed her a flashlight, then pulled others from one of the bags.

"Look!" Edwinna called over her shoulder. "I have lights! Come and help."

Movement in the darkness, then several people Tony recognized slightly made their way carefully to them. Edwinna led Tony to where the serving counter had once stood, now a pile of evergreens. "Here. She's under here. She's been in and out of consciousness. Ray is a little further back. He's got some burns, too."

"Everyone else?"

"Some broken bones, cuts from flying glass. Oh, and I'm pretty sure Bernadette is in labor. You remember her, very pregnant mom with the toddler? She's not complaining, but she's not feeling too good. We've got her in the corner away from the glass."

"When's she due?"

"Any time, she said. Have you ever delivered a baby?" Edwinna asked hopefully.

"Twice. How about you?"

"Only my own, so I think it's a little different."

"Not really. There's a birthing kit in the biggest duffel. Why don't you get it out, just in case, while I work on Donna and Ray?" He turned to the young man beside Edwinna. "You, what's your name?"

"Julio."

"Okay, Julio, come with me. As I cut off the tree limbs, you pull them back out of the way."

Tony dropped to his knees and eased under the first set of branches, sawing a path and crawling along the wet floor. Not far in, Donna was on her side, one arm at an odd angle, and the heavy limb resting on her hips. He shone his light around. Most of the impact had landed on the counter top and smashed it.

"Donna! Donna! Can you hear me?" He tried to illuminate her face without shining the light in her eyes. He touched her shoulder gently and her eyes opened, peering out from under the jackets placed to protect her from the rain pouring in the open roof.

"Tony! How did you get here? I'm stuck…." Tears filled her eyes.

"What hurts?"

"My arm, I think it's broken. There's pressure on my legs, but I can move my toes and my feet a little. My hip hurts where it's caught. My shoulder got whacked pretty hard. I turned to protect my head."

"Okay. Well, let me find out what's on top of you and check on the cook, then I'll get you out."

"Is Edwinna still okay? Everyone else?"

"I think so. A baby might be on the way—Bernadette."

“Tell Edwinna if she can get to the big closets in the hallway, going towards the Sunday School rooms, the emergency earthquake supplies are in there,” Donna spoke in short phrases, obviously in pain. “Blankets, water, flashlights, some medical supplies. If there’s anything left of the hallway, that is….”

Julio repeated the news to Edwinna. Reassured by Tony’s arrival and granted vision again with the flashlights, Edwinna began to organize the ambulatory to find and distribute the supplies, did a second round of triage, and calmed the frightened children. The able-bodied used the heaviest tables to make another layer of shelter in the most protected corner of the room, and they helped the injured to it.

Meanwhile, Tony and Julio quickly removed the limbs trapping Donna and Ray. Edwinna came back and handed him medical supplies as he splinted Donna’s arm, then the cook’s leg. They agreed that with no other apparent serious injuries, both could be carefully pulled to a safer, drier space, as the dangling roof above them swayed ominously with each wind gust.

No sooner were Donna and Ray settled than some intense cries started from the far corner, where Bernadette was huddled between the tables. Tony accompanied Edwinna and surveyed the young mother. Dee and Dwight Thomas, a volunteer couple he had met briefly before, comforted her.

“It’s coming,” Bernadette said to them between gasps. “I really have to push. I’ve been trying not to, but, oh—” Her pants and underwear lay beside her and she had just a blanket over her legs.

“I have everything ready right here,” Edwinna said to him.

“Okay,” Tony got down on his knees. “Something to clean our hands?”

Edwinna tore open a towelette pack for each of them.

“Here are some gloves, too.”

Tony asked Dwight to get behind Bernadette and prop her up a bit, and for Dee to come around and help with Bernadette’s legs. Edwinna prepared the foil emergency covering and a tiny receiving blanket for the baby, and scissors and a tie for the umbilical cord.

“Let’s get this clean sheet under you,” Tony said gently, unwrapping the large paper pad from the duffel. “The next time you’re between contractions, lift up and I’ll slide it under.” Dee helped him get Bernadette situated, and then he carefully pulled the blanket back from her knees. Edwinna focused her flashlight for him, and an unmistakable dark blotch of hair was readily apparent.

Dee gave an audible gasp.

“Are you okay?” Tony asked her.

“Yes, I’m sorry. I’ll do whatever you need.”

"I can see the head," Tony said calmly to Bernadette. "We're ready now, so push when you have to."

"My first baby came really fast," Bernadette said through gritted teeth. "Oh—"

"You're okay, here we go." With Dwight supporting her back and Edwinna and Dee each holding a leg, it only took one more push before the baby boy was delivered into Tony's hands. Suctioning the baby's mouth quickly, he was relieved when a healthy first cry burst forth. He tied and cut the cord, then snuggled the gooey infant up across his mother's chest under her shirt, skin to skin. Edwinna folded the blankets around them both while Tony waited for the afterbirth. Dee cleaned up the little head a bit, as Bernadette gently stroked him. Another woman appeared with Bernadette's toddler Cynthia, who inspected her new brother, then promptly fell asleep in Dwight's arms, one arm dangling across her mother's chest.

"Good job," Tony patted Edwinna's shoulder lightly as they headed back to Donna.

"You, too," her voice trembled. Tony maintained his touch until she had composed herself. "I'm sorry. It's just, in the midst of this huge mess, all this destruction, to have a little new life arrive. And he's perfect. It's a miracle."

"Yup. Under normal circumstances, it's a process that shouldn't need too much intercession. Been happening for a long time." Nonchalance aside, Tony was secretly pleased that this time, it had gone right.

With some effort, Donna and the cook had been moved to safer quarters, blankets stuffed around them to soften the hard floor. Tony kneeled so he was closer to Donna's eye level. He checked again to be sure she was settled comfortably for the night.

"I'm sorry, I have to go help get the roads open. But everyone's in good shape here. Mom and baby are doing fine. It's a boy, by the way. Edwinna's got everything under control."

"Thank you for coming for us," Donna talked softly, happy she had finally found a way to prop her arm, shoulder and hip so they didn't hurt as much.

Tony leaned forward and kissed her gently on the forehead. She grabbed his shirt with her good hand and pulled him closer for a minute, just to feel his cheek on hers.

"I'll be back as soon as I can," he promised. "It might be twenty-four hours or more. If you get to the hospital, I'll find you, don't worry. Oh, here's your phone. Julio came across it in the branches. I checked and your kids are fine." He pressed the black rectangle into her hand. "I'll see you soon."

Donna leaned back and closed her eyes, awash in the realization that she had fallen totally, head-over-heels in love with a first responder.

Tony parked the Hummer in what remained of the north end fire station parking lot. Both fire engines sat at the curb, but couldn't get anywhere because of the downed trees. A large crew was working on clearing the roadway.

Emergency lights cast an odd pall over the institutional gray walls inside the building. Tony surveyed the gathered responders and picked out the captain.

"Tony Wagner," he introduced himself. "Military first response. You've got a hundred people in the social hall of the church on 147th with three trees through the roof. Two people with serious fractures and a young mother with a newborn, everyone else not too bad, a few more broken bones. But the roads are tough."

"That's our problem, we can't get anywhere. And the storm's not over, we can't call for civilians to go clear their streets for at least another two hours."

"How can I help?"

"What are you driving? How'd you get through?"

"I've got a Hummer out front."

This was the first good news the captain had received all evening.

"Okay, we know the neighborhood at the top of the hill got hit hard. All those old Douglas firs came down. If you could get two medical teams up there, there's about fifteen houses that need help. Get the crews as far as you can, do triage. We'll find some guys to go with you to start clearing the road from the top down. Try to make a staging area. Let's see how much stuff we can pack in your vehicle."

Half-an-hour later Tony was laboriously guiding the Hummer over the tree-covered roads to the Hilltop neighborhood, shocked at the path of destruction on the slope. Finally hitting an impassable section a third of a mile from the top, he left one crew to clear the road. Helping the two EMT teams haul their stuff on foot up the last five hundred yards, he bemoaned the fact that his exercise program with Donna had not taken off a bit more excess weight.

Seventy-two hours later, Tony sank into his brown leather, man-cave sofa, his one nod to ridiculously masculine furniture in his modest home. He was tired. Days of helping to clear roads and transport the injured had exhausted him. Twice he'd caught a few hours of sleep on a cot at the fire station, but the guest mattress was not particularly comfortable for someone of his bulk and aging back.

His computer was set up on the coffee table before him, a candid picture of Donna looking lovely among her flowers on the screensaver. He realized it had been nearly six weeks since he had checked her day planner.

Why was that? Because now she told him her schedule. Now they talked every day, often two or three times.

Liz's cautions rang through his head. Donna most likely would not take it well to know that he had accessed her computer. Even if it seemed justified at the time, at least to him. Things were going so well, he knew he should not jeopardize their relationship. Liz's stern look came to mind. He didn't need the information now, he convinced himself. He had won Donna over, and her son and daughters, too. When he had brought her home from the hospital in the Hummer this morning, he'd given the kids a ride around the block. Her son had seemed especially impressed. His low life father with the baby-faced girlfriend might drive a truck, but he sure didn't have a Hummer.

Tony brought up his computer programs, found the spyware, and clicked through the necessary steps to remove it. The final "Are you sure you want to uninstall SPY5?" displayed. His finger hesitated. He really should. The benefits so outweighed the risks of discovery. Would Liz not say this was a critical moment, a chance to make the right choice when so often before he had made the wrong one? Was this the start of a new day or not?

The jangle of his phone startled him…Donna's ring tone, of all things. Without hesitation, his hovering finger did the right thing as he put the phone to his ear.

"So you uninstalled your spy ware?" For once Liz had a smile on her face, slowly fading when Tony did not immediately respond.

"I did uninstall it," his tone was placating yet somewhat unrepentant, "but I reinstalled it later that afternoon."

"Tony!" Her aggravation overcame her usual calm, accepting demeanor.

"Because," he continued before she could get started, "I might need it sometime for an emergency. Nothing to do with Donna. I deleted everything on my computer that had anything to do with her if I had come by it without her knowledge. Now I only have her emails and a few photos she's sent. I even deleted the surreptitious pictures I took, including my most favorite of her standing among the flowers. But she didn't know I took it, so I dumped it. Really, now everything is completely above board as far as Donna is concerned. Honest."

"How many pictures were there?" Liz's heart had taken a sudden lurch.

"Four. Only four. She was showing me her workshop after one of our first dates and she looked so pretty among the flowers, I snapped a couple with my phone when she wasn't looking."

Liz's face was set in an unhappy look.

"I wasn't hiding in the bushes with a telephoto lens or anything. Honest."

Liz observed him sternly while trying to decide if she believed him. He had always been a man of his word. *Almost* always.

"Look, I only hacked her computer so I could bump into her," he continued earnestly. "I had no way to contact her. After our May adventure to rescue you, she changed her appointment day because of the new business. I had no way to arrange an accidental meeting."

"'Arrange an accidental meeting.' Does anything in that sentence sound wrong to you?"

"You know what I mean. You certainly weren't going to give me any personal information about your client. The nursery wouldn't tell me anything. I was stuck."

Liz looked into his calm, steady eyes and then sighed, reconciling the fact that, despite ten years of effort on her part, this intelligent former Marine's interpersonal skills might require continued coaching.

"Tell me about your parents. How was it, being in Boston this time?"

Tony thought of his mother, of sitting in the library with her each evening after dinner, making plans for the next day that would never come to fruition. Of how she refused to let the world close in on her too tightly, despite his father's failing health and her own undependable body. Of how she teased him about a new "girlfriend" and bragged about his ex-wives' children, as if they were grandchildren of her own. He thought about driving through that intersection ever so carefully, holding his breath until he reached the other side.

"Better, I think. This time was definitely a little better."

Chapter Six: Liz Brubaker, M.A.

October, 2011—May, 2012

The hurried sound of Liz's footsteps in the hallway put Tony on alert. Fifteen minutes late, he was further concerned when she arrived at the door. Hair in disarray, purse unzipped, her glasses nearly falling out, and red eyes all signaled trouble.

"I'm sorry I'm late, Tony." She didn't break stride as she moved past the waiting room without inviting him to follow. "Give me one more minute."

He sat patiently—patient waiting was his trademark, after all—until Liz returned to fetch him, now pulled together and freshened up.

Lowering himself into his favorite chair in her office, he studied his counselor carefully. Roles were reversed today; it was Liz who could not meet his eyes as she began her opening routine.

"What is it, Liz?" he finally interrupted. "What's happened?"

She shook her head. "A family matter, that's all. Don't worry about it."

"Can I help in some way?"

"No, I'll take care of it."

And that was that until Liz called him late on Friday night.

"I might need your help," Liz spoke quietly. "I don't know where to turn."

"What's going on?"

"Could we meet at my office? Even though it's late?"

"Or," Tony assumed all ethical behavior was possibly going out the window, "I could come to your house."

Thirty minutes later, with two cups of steaming decaf in a cardboard carry tray and his ever-present computer case slung over his shoulder, Tony let himself through the front gate and walked up the steps to Liz's porch.

"This is awkward," she began, gratefully holding the warm cup in her hands as she perched on the overstuffed couch. Devoid of even the little make-up she usually wore and in casual clothes instead of her professional attire, Liz appeared particularly vulnerable.

"You know you can tell me anything," Tony tried to coax a smile by using her favorite phrase.

"It's a bit embarrassing." Liz stared into her cup. "And frightening, too. I'm being blackmailed." Her voice dropped.

Tony's eyebrows, rather bushy compared to his partially bald head, shot up. "Blackmailed? By whom?"

"My ex. Lloyd."

"Lloyd? But you haven't seen him in what, ten years?"

"At least. But he has something I want very badly." Her eyes filled with tears. "My sister's address."

"Really." Completely intrigued, Tony wiped his forehead as the hot coffee warmed him a little too much. A ransom demand had not been what he had expected at all. Trouble with a client or a clandestine affair gone bad, maybe yes. But ransom?

"So you and your sister are estranged, then?"

"Not exactly. I lost her. I moved away from Portland when I was 18 and Ginger was only 12. With my parents both alcoholics, things were quite bad for me. More for me than for her, so I thought she'd be okay till I could get her out. I was going to find a job and save some money, then go back. I thought it would take a couple months, but it took a year." Liz stopped to wipe the increasing tears. A minute passed before she could begin again. "When I returned, she'd run away. I tried and tried to find her on the street, but I couldn't. My parents' health declined and they each died. Eventually I moved up here, married and went to school. You know the rest."

"How does Lloyd figure into this?"

Liz stood and paced to the windows and back, recounting the unforeseen phone call from Lloyd the previous week, announcing he had found Ginger. For $25,000 he would put Liz in touch with her. Liz would gladly pay that amount, but Lloyd had been untrustworthy in the past, cooking up a myriad of schemes to support his gambling habit.

"Do you have *any* idea where they might be?" Tony inquired thoughtfully.

"Probably not Oregon, and early on I'd searched Washington and California pretty thoroughly, too." Liz sank back onto the sofa. "I gave up a bit after the first fifteen years."

"What do you want me to do?" Tony set his coffee cup on the end table.

"Work some electronic magic. See if Lloyd's on the level. Find out where Ginger is and if she's okay."

"How long do you have?"

"Only a week, till he leaves for Mexico—a business opportunity."

"Okay. Do you have a phone number for him? How are you supposed to contact him?"

"He'll call me…on a blocked line."

"How did he get *your* number?"

"Brubaker is my family name. I've kept it professionally, and the house phone listed that way, in case Ginger was trying to find me."

"All right, give me all the details you have about him…and her. Maybe some pictures? I'll see what I can do."

By tracing Liz's incoming calls compliments of his friends in the police department, Tony had some news at his Monday appointment.

"Lloyd's in Spokane. Been there at least ten years."

"And Ginger?" Liz had spent the weekend bouncing wildly from hope that her sister had been found to despair that this was just another of her ex-husband's scams.

"Not sure. I'm driving to Spokane this afternoon. I should know something in a few days."

"Don't go, Tony. I should never have gotten you involved. I'll go to the police…even though he said if I did I'd never see Ginger again."

"Don't worry. I'll be very discreet. And the police already know. My buddy opened a file for us. It'll give me some help in Spokane…if I need it."

Liz paced her front porch, anxiously looking down the street, the cell phone in her hand ready to be flipped open at the first ring.

"Hello?" she nearly shouted when the call came.

"We're almost there. Turning onto Sunset now." Liz peered down the street, then saw Tony's black SUV come into view. Her heart was beating so hard it made her teeth ache. Finally, the car stopped in front of her house. Tony popped out of his side, came around to the rear passenger door, and opened it. By then, Liz was on the sidewalk, anxiously watching as Tony fiddled with the latch of the car seat. In the next seconds, he was lifting a brown-haired, brown-eyed, thumb-sucking four-year-old out onto the grass. She had a firm grip on a discolored stuffed animal that had probably been a dog at one time.

"Chloe, this is your Aunt Liz. Liz, here's Chloe."

Liz squatted down to the child's eye level and murmured softly, "Hello, Chloe. I'm so glad you're here."

The child looked at her with big eyes and backed up a step, leaning against Tony's legs.

"Would you like to come in and meet my dog? He wants to meet you. And I've got a snack ready for you, if you like."

"We stopped on the way for some lunch, but I'm hungry again. How about you, Chloe? Shall I get your things and we can go in and meet the dog?" Tony patted the child's thin shoulder reassuringly.

Liz extended her hand, and Chloe reached for it. Overwhelmed, Liz fought back tears at the touch of the soft skin and the small fingers wrapped around hers. Tony retrieved two suitcases and followed them into the house.

"She doesn't talk much," Tony explained, as they observed Chloe toss the ball for Poochie in the back yard.

"Were there any medical records in the final paperwork? When the social worker first called, she wasn't sure if Chloe had ever seen a pediatrician."

"There's not much, Children's Services was just starting to sort it all out." Tony recounted the events leading up to Ginger's arrest: After being fired for stealing from her employer, she tried to disappear and was living in her car with Chloe. An officer ran the plate when the dilapidated vehicle was parked too long in one spot and found the warrant. Ginger contacted Lloyd, whom she had met in one of her rehab stints, and asked him to take Chloe to Liz. Knowing from their early marriage how hard Liz had tried to find Ginger, he apparently sensed a business opportunity he couldn't pass up.

"Your sister looks a lot like you, by the way. Strong family resemblance. She's changed her name several times, lived back East for quite a while, that's why you couldn't find her."

"You're sure Chloe's father died?"

"Yup. I ordered a copy of the death certificate for you. I think Ginger might have made it if not for losing Grant." Although it was rather rare to die of appendicitis, the family had no health care and waited too long to go to the ER when Grant became ill. "It's a shame, they made a nice little family. The good news is that I think after being busted the one time after he died, your sister has managed to stay clean and sober for three years, not easy with your family background. Her mistake was turning to stealing from her employer to make the rent."

Liz was filled with such murderous anger at her ex-husband for jeopardizing this little girl she could barely contain herself. Tony noticed the tightening of her jaw.

"It's okay. She's safe here with you. Nothing's going to happen to her now."

Chloe finished playing and came back to them.

"Ready for a peanut butter and jelly sandwich?" Liz couldn't get enough of looking at the smaller version of her sister's face.

Chloe's eyes brightened and she scampered up the back steps behind the dog.

Stocking feet up in her comfortable recliner, Liz contentedly observed the chaos of her living room. Paige, her younger daughter, had fallen asleep at one end of the couch with Chloe snuggled against her. Marcia, the older, had just closed her eyes at the other. Eager to meet the cousin they never knew existed, the girls had arrived from Portland early on Saturday. Chloe's first trip ever to a zoo was followed by movie night at home. The sisters had brought new toys which were spread out in groups: A doll house family had taken up residence beside the red armchair; an entire zoo stretched across the floor in front of the sofa; and a castle-shaped tower of connecting blocks stood sentry by the door. Sticky remnants of flameless s'mores—graham crackers, chocolate syrup and marshmallow fluff—covered the coffee table. Liz had borrowed two DVDs from Mark's house, where Chloe was spending her days with five-year-old Junie until formal child care could be arranged. Halfway through the second show fifty percent of the audience was sound asleep.

The peace of the late evening had been marred only by Marcia's whispered questions about Lloyd. Liz seethed upon learning he had contacted his daughters to offer a good return on whatever money they would like to invest in his latest business venture. Both girls called their father "Llo-yd," pronounced in two drawn-out syllables with derision, ever since he had gone missing and then announced himself on the phone as "It's Lloyd," not recognizing his own daughter's thirteen-year-old voice. Careful to speak of him only in neutral terms, Liz nevertheless felt no need to attempt repair of the broken relationships his failures and absences had created.

After Paige and Chloe fell asleep, Marcia grilled her mother about a previously undiscussed aspect of the marriage: How she could have fallen in love with Lloyd in the first place and failed to see where he was headed? Liz knew both daughters were anxious not to repeat their parents' mistakes, and she tried to answer honestly and accept blame where it was due. But it was hard to explain why, upon leaving home and so desperate for independence, she had attached herself so fiercely to anyone, even a seemingly steady guy, someone who had loved, protected, and supported her after she'd grown up too fast, raising herself and her sister Ginny. The marriage had been happy at first, but Lloyd's social drinking drifted into heavier drinking and other bad habits. When he finally lost his job, the family's finances had spiraled downwards with frightening rapidity. Liz had managed to get her Masters in Counseling once the girls started school, and then slowly and steadily removed the three of them from the marriage. The experience might have made her a more sympathetic therapist, but she was forever sorry for the trauma it had caused her daughters.

The news began on the muted, closed-captioned TV; she'd wait for the weather and then shepherd everyone to bed.

The house felt full and vibrant again. Liz had missed the quiet heartbeat of her family within its walls.

Three weeks later, on a cool and crisp Saturday morning in November, Liz was moving a load of towels from the washer to the dryer when she glanced in the back yard and then did a double-take. No Chloe. And no dog.

Out the door and down the porch stairs, the sight of the open gate made her stomach drop. Calling Chloe's name, Liz ran into the alley but could not see her anywhere. Increasingly frantic, she ran through the side yard, calling for both the dog and Chloe. Back into the house for her car keys, she drove up and down the street calling, but no one was in view.

"Hey, Liz. What's up?"

"Tony—Chloe's gone. She opened the gate in the backyard while I was changing the laundry." Liz choked back tears and continued desperately searching the street as she talked.

"Okay, take a breath, I'm sure she hasn't gone far. How long ago?"

"Twenty minutes. I've gone up and down the block and already called the police, they're coming. But Tony, the beach—" Liz's voice broke.

"I'm forty-five minutes away. Stay put, do what the police tell you to do, I'll be there as soon as I can. She's probably right around the corner. She's a pretty independent little kid, you know. On her own a lot."

"What if someone took her?" Liz could barely form the words.

"I think that's unlikely. I'll be there as soon as I can."

"How could she get out of sight so fast?" Liz looked up the street again as a police cruiser came into view.

Tony scrolled through his contacts as he drove.

"Roberta? It's Tony Wagner." There was silence on the other end. "From Liz's office?"

"Don't worry, I remember! I was just surprised to see your name. I haven't seen you since May."

"Listen, it's a long story, but Liz needs help badly. I'm in the south end of the city and can't get there for forty-five minutes, but I thought of you since you live a lot closer and you know where she lives."

"What's happened?"

"Three weeks ago Liz became the guardian for her little niece, four years old. She's wandered out of the yard and Liz is a mess. The police are coming, but she needs someone with her. Could you go?"

"I can leave right now."

"So she's been with you how long?" The young officer had his notepad out.

"Three weeks." Liz fretfully paced, watching every movement on the street.

"Her parents?"

"Father's dead. My sister is in jail in Spokane."

"Anyone else who would have an interest in the child? The father's parents?"

"I don't think so, but I don't know for sure. You think it's an abduction?"

The officer shook his head. "I think she's wandered off with your dog, but I have to ask. Anyone else with an interest in the child?"

"I don't think so." Liz thought of Lloyd. But Tony said that was all taken care of. She'd wait to ask him before mentioning it. "Oh, and she doesn't talk much. I don't think she'd ever ask anyone for help. She's only in her thin jacket, nothing very warm to be out this long." Tears were welling up and she had to fight to control them.

"Do you have a picture?"

Liz realized miserably that she didn't. Marcia had taken some pictures at the zoo on her phone, but there wasn't anything readily available in the house.

Two neighbors appeared, alerted by the sight of the police cars, and now they each took a different direction to search on foot. Liz watched another police car slowly go through the intersection at the end of the street. *Oh, Chloe, where are you?*

"Poochie! Poochie! Come home!" she called as loudly as she could.

"Liz."

Liz turned abruptly. "Roberta. What are you doing here?"

"Tony called. What can I do?"

"He told you? I never thought she'd be able to open that gate, the latch sticks terribly."

"Four-year-olds are remarkably adept when they want to be."

"What should I do?" Liz asked forlornly. "The police want me to stay here but I want to go looking."

"How about the house? Have you checked it top to bottom?"

"They were going to have an officer do it after they did the first quick search through the neighborhood."

"All right, why don't I start there? Any secret hiding spaces? Attic?"

"She'd never be able to get up there, it's a pull-down ladder in the upstairs hall. There's a little bit of a crawl space under the house, but the entrance is locked."

Roberta was checking the large walk-in closet on the second floor when her cell phone jangled and showed Tony's number.

"Hi, Tony."

"How are things?"

"Nothing yet. I'm searching the house. The police are doing loops around the neighborhood. Some neighbor friends are going door to door."

"Liz isn't picking up her phone. Could you go tell her two things? Either the dog's following Chloe, or Chloe's following the dog. Ask her where they walk the dog each day, and someone should go do that route. And the other thing is, I think Chloe's afraid of the police. It was the police who took her when she was living in the car and she didn't see her mom again after that. So if it's uniformed police officers looking, she's probably not going to come out."

Liz listened thoughtfully as Roberta repeated Tony's message.

"We walk the dog around the block after dinner, but on weekends we go to the beach, which Poochie loves. So they might have gone that way." The police officer standing with her relayed the new information into his shoulder mike.

"Which way is the beach access?" Roberta tugged her jacket closer. "I could head that direction."

"Down to the end of the block, then go right. Go about two more blocks and then there's a path through the woods. They've sent officers, but maybe she's hiding. Call the dog…he'll remember you. But maybe I should go." Liz's was having trouble keeping her thoughts from bouncing wildly from one frightening scenario to the next.

"I think you should stay here. And Tony said your cell phone isn't on."

Liz glanced at her phone, which she'd been tightly gripping throughout. "Oh, gosh, I've got the volume down."

"Okay, I'm heading to the beach. There's an officer searching inside now, so that'll be covered. I don't think she's there, though, because where would Poochie be?"

Twenty more minutes passed. Finally, Tony's black SUV turned the corner.

"Climb in," he yelled, rolling to a stop. "City Animal Control just got a call about a dog acting erratically on the beach. Fits Poochie's description. Come on, I'll drive you."

Liz turned to the officer.

"Got it," he said into his radio as he waved her on, "she's on her way."

Tony carefully navigated the twisty road down to the beach, drove up the access path by the cabana, maneuvered over the bendable pylons blocking the emergency lane, and then headed onto the sand.

"Are you allowed to do this?"

"I doubt it. They said south of 190th, must be down that way." The SUV jolted over the wood debris and rocks. "Look, there's Roberta coming through the woods."

"Who said what, and how did you hear about it?"

"I was monitoring calls to Animal Control…and one came in about a dog acting oddly and seemingly alone on the beach."

"What if she's gone in the water?" Liz frantically searched the shore break, afraid of seeing a blotch of colored jacket.

"I don't think so. Look, there's Poochie, by those logs."

Over the summer, a shelter had been built above the tide line by propping bleached logs against each other. Poochie was running back and forth in front of the haphazard teepee, barking. A police officer was making no headway getting past the dog who growled whenever he came too close.

"Poochie!" Liz bounded out the car door. "Poochie, come!"

The dog ran to her, leaping up and then racing back to the teepee. On his next excited run to Liz, Tony grabbed and held him. The officer got to the shelter only a few steps ahead of Liz.

"She's here," he called.

A forlorn-looking ball of clothing was pressed into the shadows.

"Chloe, it's okay," Liz quietly spoke as she stooped down and entered the darkness. "Come on, sweetie; it's okay. Everyone's looking for you."

Chloe came to her aunt's embrace, trembling.

"Chloe," Liz held her close, "I was so scared."

"I was okay. I had Poochie with me."

Liz hugged her tighter, then realized these were the first complete sentences the child had said in three weeks.

"I want my mommy," Chloe whispered, leaning against her aunt.

"I know you do, honey. I know you do. We'll work on that. Say, that Poochie sure is a good friend. But why did you two leave the yard?" Liz stroked the short brown hair.

"The ball went over the fence. So we went to get it, then Poochie ran away. So I went to get him. I thought you'd be mad if I lost him."

"I'd only be mad if I lost YOU." Liz fought back tears. "Well, let's go get warmed up at home, shall we?"

"Well, another happy ending," Roberta said, admiring the interior of the fully loaded SUV as she caught a ride with Tony back to her own car. "Interesting things certainly seem to happen when I'm around you." Roberta thought back to the day in Liz's waiting room when Tony handed her his business card, neatly printed with only his name and a phone number. "If you don't mind my asking, what is it, exactly, that you do for a living?"

"Consulting and emergency response," Tony replied casually, carefully following the patrol car carrying Liz and Chloe.

Roberta did not have the slightest idea what Tony's answer meant, but she clearly understood no further explanation would be forthcoming.

Liz sank into the most comfortable chair in Mark's office early Monday morning.

"I can't believe I lost her. After all the terrible things I've thought about people who can't keep track of their kids, I take my eye off her for two minutes and I lose her. Two minutes, Mark, honest, one minute they were in the yard, two minutes later she was gone."

"Don't beat yourself up too much. It's been twenty years since you've had to watch a preschooler. And she arrived without much notice."

"That's no excuse. You and Hope make it look effortless. Being able to leave her at your house until I find daycare is a godsend. I'm going to be sorry to move her, she loves Junie so."

"We'll cross that bridge when we come to it. How are things going with her mom?"

"I've hired a Spokane attorney for her. Ginny was only stealing enough to help pay the rent, and she'd been a good employee before that, but her employer is pretty angry. At least she's stayed clean and sober." The clouds parted a bit and sun shone through the window onto Liz's cheek. She turned her head toward the warmth and closed her eyes.

"What are you thinking right now?"

Liz turned back and shook her head. "What a bad job I did raising her. What a terrible mistake it was not to take her with me when I left."

"Have you been able to talk with her about that?"

"No. We've spoken on the phone twice for a few minutes, but it's been all about Chloe. I wouldn't know where to start."

"Here." Mark pulled over a straight-backed chair. "Pretend she's sitting here and talk to her."

"You know I don't do empty chair work in my practice." The Gestalt technique had always seemed somewhat contrived to her.

"Try it. Can't hurt, might help. What do you want to say to her?"

After several more protests, Liz sat quietly. Five different sentences formed in her head before she could get one out.

"I would say, I'm sorry."

"Don't talk to me, talk to her," Mark nodded toward the empty chair.

"I'm sorry." Liz squared her shoulders, facing her imaginary sister. "I'm sorry I didn't take you when I left. I thought you'd be okay for a couple months and I'd come back for you as soon I got settled. I didn't know it would take so long." Silence.

"Okay, now switch seats, and be your sister talking to you."

"Mark, honestly—"

"Come on. You can do it."

Liz reluctantly switched seats. She closed her eyes and tried to become her sister. Feelings of sadness and despair washed over her and tears welled in her eyes.

“You left me,” she said quietly. “I wanted you to take me, but you left me.”

After another moment of silence, Mark pointed his finger, indicating Liz should switch. She took her own seat again.

“I tried to find you. I did everything I could. If you hadn’t run away, I would have gotten you. Why did you run away?”

Switch. Liz imagined what it must have been like in that household.

“It was so much worse without you. They were drunk all the time. The bills piled up. Dad started hitting…Mom, me, the walls, the dog. I had to leave. And you didn’t tell me where you had gone! *I couldn’t find you.*”

Switch. *I couldn’t find you.* That hard truth had finally been unwrapped in Liz’s heart. Ginny hadn’t run *away from* home, she had been running *to* Liz. But Liz hadn’t wanted anyone to know where she was—not even her sister. Being found would have meant being forced by guilt to return home. So badly had she needed to be away from that toxic environment, she’d sacrificed her sister to do it: an uncomfortable and alarming realization.

A steely resolve settled over Liz’s shoulders like an invincible cloak. *Well, amends could be made. Amends could most certainly be made.*

“Thanks, Mark.” Liz met her good friend’s kind eyes as she rose to meet her first client.

“Don’t thank me. Thank the chair.”

“Hey, Mark.” With the phone to her ear, Liz indelicately swallowed a mouthful of pancake. “What’s up?”

“Are you and Chloe dressed yet?”

“Not quite.” Lost in thought as Chloe colored at the kitchen table across from her, Liz had been pondering how to reunite Chloe with her mother if, in fact, Ginger received a reduced sentence with her plea bargain. “Why?”

“In about fifteen minutes a truck is going to arrive at your back gate. Go get some clothes on. We’ll be there in ten.”

“We? Who’s we? What’s going on?”

“Go get dressed, unless you want to be flapping around for all the world to see in your nightgown. This is a good thing, I promise.”

In nine minutes flat, Liz and Chloe had pulled on clothes and stood watching the alley. At the sound of the doorbell, Chloe ran to the front.

Mark, his wife Hope, nine-year-old Max, and five-year-old Junie were clustered on the porch amongst the Christmas decorations, trying to look subdued but having difficulty.

"Hey, everyone, what's going on?" Liz loved Mark's family dearly, but they had never dropped in so early on a weekend before.

"We have a surprise for Chloe!" Junie shouted exuberantly. "A happy, happy surprise!"

Chloe looked at them quizzically, as no one carried a package. Now the sound of a truck came from the back of the house.

"I'll go unlock the gate," Mark told Liz. "You put Poochie somewhere safe. No escapes today."

"Mark, enough now. What's happening?" A bit exasperated, Liz followed the family through the house after shooing Poochie into the laundry room and closing the door.

Mark fiddled with the new locking gate latch. The rear door of the truck rolled up, and Liz found herself staring at large sections of brightly painted wood.

"Where do you want it?" the lead delivery man asked her. The driver and two female workers surveyed her yard.

"I'd put it there," the taller woman pointed to a corner that got good morning sun.

"What is it? A playhouse?" The shape became evident as the pieces came off the truck. "You bought Chloe a playhouse?" Liz was momentarily too shocked to comprehend. Agreeing to the corner spot, Liz watched the crew prepare the base area and then bolt the walls together. Chloe stood with her mouth open in amazement as not a simple cottage but a real house, complete with loft, windows, and doors, speedily manifested itself before her.

Liz rejoined Mark and Hope on the porch.

"It's a lovely surprise. But how we can accept it? These cost upward of five thousand dollars! I know, because I've looked at them!"

"It's so Chloe can feel like she has a place of her own." Mark used his calm, professional, counseling voice. "Important for this transitional time, don't you think?"

"Of course, but the money—"

"We got one for Junie, too." This time his eyes sparkled as he waited for her reaction.

Liz took a step back and looked at her good—but notoriously thrifty—friend and his equally economically-minded wife. "I don't understand."

"It's been so hard to keep a secret from you, Liz. But we won the lottery last month." Mark's arm encircled his wife as they watched Liz's face together.

"What?" The explanation simply would not compute in her head.

"We won the lottery," he repeated. "Not the huge Powerball one, but one of the smaller ones. Five million, three after taxes."

"I didn't even know you played," Liz managed to sputter.

"Neither did I," Hope finally spoke, "but turns out, every once in a while, if he was at the store and the odds were good, he'd pick up a ticket. We were in shock for the first 24 hours. I couldn't believe it."

"Remember that Monday I came in so late?" Mark glanced in the yard to check on the kids. "When I barely spoke to you? It was that weekend. I felt like I was going to blurt it out at any moment!"

"Do you have a plan?"

"All set up. We're good to get the kids through college, put some toward retirement, have a little extra spending money now, and decide on a really good idea to do with the rest." His delight was infectious.

"And our practice?"

"I'll keep seeing clients, of course! I wouldn't give that up."

There were squeals in the yard as Chloe, led by Junie and Max, helped the delivery crew haul in the final items: a miniature refrigerator and stove complete with pots, pans, and dishes; a table and four chairs; a small green couch; and a little bed that looked like it had come straight from a fairy tale, canopy and all.

Later that day, Liz perched carefully on one of the petite chairs, sipping apple juice and nibbling an egg salad sandwich from a bright yellow plate. Chloe had brought her stuffed animals and dolls out to join the party.

"Maybe Mommy can live here," Chloe said, pouring more juice from the flowered teapot with an unsteady hand. "You can live in your house, and Mommy and I can live here."

"Maybe," Liz replied with a gentle smile. "I'm working on it, honey, I'm working on it."

"Aunt Liz, look! There's that man. He's looking at us."

Liz stopped loading the car with the gorgeous spring annuals she and Chloe had picked out and let her eyes follow Chloe's pointing finger across the parking lot.

Tony Wagner and Donna Noyes were locking their bikes up at the entrance to the garden center. Liz was impressed. Donna's house must be at least ten miles down the community bike trail, but the popular nursery and café would be a perfect destination for anyone who loved flowers on this sunny March afternoon.

Tony was looking in Liz's direction and gave a nod as if he was waiting to know her next move.

"Do you want to go say hello?" Liz asked Chloe. "That's Tony Wagner, do you remember? He brought you to me. And helped find you on the beach when Poochie ran away."

"I know."

"Shall we go say hi?"

Chloe thought about it a minute.

"No. I'm hungry. Let's go home and get lunch."

When Liz looked back, Donna and Tony had disappeared inside. As she finished loading the car, Liz considered the bewildering peculiarities of love. She had been worried about the relationship between those two from the beginning, but other than firmly cautioning each to *take it slowly*, she was doing her best to stay out of it.

Two months later, Tony came into her office and slumped into the chair across from Liz, his slimming body a puddle of despair.

"It's over."

"What's over?" Shocked at his appearance, Liz had never seen him so dejected.

"Donna."

Liz waited for more.

"She found out. About the divorce. And the church. Everything. She's furious."

"I'm so sorry." Liz sighed and tried not to scream, *I told you so*. "But you realized the risks."

Silence. Tony stared at the carpet.

"Women in the midst of bad divorces can't be treated like some kind of military salvage exercise."

"I thought I was being helpful."

Silence again.

"How did she find out?"

"An unfortunate coincidence," Tony sighed. "Taffy made a phone call when she was drunk one night complaining about having so little money to live on since the settlement and blaming Donna. Then the next week, Donna overheard a conversation at church about the miraculous timing of the anonymous gift, with the daycare starting and all, and something got her wheels turning. She approached a friend on the finance committee and learned the money had come from the Endicott Foundation. Researching that brought it back to my door step."

"I'm surprised you left such an obvious money trail from the church to you."

"The money had to come from somewhere. Too clandestine and it would have seemed suspicious." He sighed again miserably.

"Oh, Tony." It was hard not to be sympathetic in the face of such desolation. "I suppose this is why Donna cancelled her appointment this week." *Rather tersely, in fact,* Liz remembered.

Tony shrugged.

"You've apologized?"

"She won't take my calls. I sent a big basket of fruit. She threw it out on the front lawn. The birds enjoyed it immensely."

"And you know this because?"

"I've driven past the house a few times."

"Tony! That's it! Look me in the eye, now," Liz's usually controlled temper got the better of her. "I know you're hurting, but I forbid you to go anywhere near her—physically or electronically. You can work on a letter explaining yourself and expressing how remorseful you are. But you are not to approach her or watch her from afar in any way, shape, or form, do I make myself clear?"

"It's not like I'm some stalker."

"From where I sit, you're pretty damn close sometimes."

"It's my training; it's what I do."

"And I will reiterate that there is not a war going on in North Seattle." Liz's voice softened a bit. "Your armed forces tactics are useless in relationship matters like this, and, in fact, they've made things worse."

"That's not what you said when you wanted me to find Ginny," Tony refuted quietly.

"That was different. And you know it," she snapped. Now she was fired up again. Her eyes bore into the top of his bent head.

"It's just, I was happy again." Tony shuffled his feet despondently. "She made me so happy. And I blew it."

Liz waited. "Give her a month," she finally suggested. "With some time, she might forgive you. But that's her choice to make, with no influence from you. Or me, for that matter."

“I really screwed up.”

Liz bit her lip; she didn’t want to show how much she agreed with that statement.

“Do you need to find an AA meeting tonight? I don’t want you to start drinking over this.”

“I’ll be okay.” Tony recovered both his composure and his military posture. “Sometimes missions go bad,” he said philosophically.

“Yes,” Liz agreed. “And sometimes people make mistakes, but it’s not the end of the world. You learn and you go on.”

“I didn’t know it could hurt this much.”

Liz recognized what a vulnerable statement that was, coming from someone trained to have no emotions.

“That hurt is good. It means you’re really feeling things, not all blocked up. Your human side is showing. People would rather connect to humans than military commanders. You’re not in the service anymore.”

They sat silently while Liz pondered why Tony had not covered his tracks better regarding the money trail. It seemed an unusual oversight for him. Was it possible he unconsciously wanted to be found out by Donna, to put an end to the deceptions? Or was he undermining the relationship, afraid of commitment? She was fairly certain this was the most serious relationship he’d had since the accident which had ended his military career over fifteen years ago.

The first years of their counseling sessions, when Tony had moved to Seattle to start fresh, had been spent dealing with the aftermath of that accident. The public story was well known in Boston: two decorated Marines returning from an evening event, slammed at high speed by a drunk driver in a pick-up truck. Tony's best friend Lou Endicott had been driving and was killed instantly. Among other injuries, Tony had suffered broken legs, a broken pelvis, and a broken arm.

The private story, the one that had scarred Tony far beyond his surgical wounds, had taken several years to get out of him: He had only survived because he was drunk himself. Lou had taken the keys and was driving Tony's car, receiving the full impact of the collision on the driver's side. Weeks in the hospital and subsequent rehab had acted as an effective detox, and Tony had remained sober ever since. He had created the Endicott Foundation from the funds received in the accident settlement and had named it for his friend.

"They were about to kick me out," Tony said quietly.

"I'm sorry?" Liz leaned forward to hear better.

"The Marines. After my second divorce, I was in Bosnia four years. Fairly miserable. When I came home, I was drinking heavily, the worst it had ever been. My unpredictable performance caught up with me, and my commander lost patience. I'd just been put on notice, but I didn't care, I blew him off. Lou was trying to talk some sense into me that night. Instead, I killed him…as much as if I'd had a gun in my hand. I should have been sober and driving the car. I was the better driver; I might have avoided the collision."

"I doubt that."

"Well, still. Either way, it wasn't the exit from the Marines I'd wanted."

At long last, this final piece of the story had surfaced. Liz had always felt there was one more blistering sore in Tony's gut that had prevented him from completely healing. Now everything made sense. Guilt from his friend's death and the shame of knowing he had been about to be discharged, probably dishonorably, from the career he loved, would have been an unbearable burden for this complicated man.

"It'll be all right," she consoled him. "You'll see, things will work out. Give it time."

But she had no absolute faith that it would be so.

Chapter Seven: Mark Fleming, Ph.D.

April—September, 2012

Liz thought she heard music coming from her office as she came down the hallway on Saturday morning, which seemed odd. She passed Mark's closed door, assuming he was in a session, as his van was parked in its usual spot out front.

Cautiously, she pushed her door open, puzzled by why the radio and lights were on, but then even more surprised because standing in the middle of her rug was a horse. A very small horse, wearing a diaper. She stared, uncertain what to do. The horse observed her wisely, giving a little head shake in apparent greeting, then barring its teeth as if smiling. Then it returned to consuming her fern. Liz pulled the door closed, shifted to the right, and knocked sharply on Mark's door. The door opened a crack.

"Liz! I didn't know you were coming in this morning."

"There's a horse in my office wearing a diaper."

"A miniature Shetland Pony, actually—"

"Mark!"

"I can explain, but I've got a client with an emergency and I had to stop here while in transit with the pony. I couldn't leave her in the van. She's only just away from her mother. Twenty more minutes, that's all I need."

Liz could hear weeping from his office.

"Pretend she's a big dog. She won't bother you at all."

"I have a big dog, Mark. She's not a big dog. She's eating my plant. Why isn't she in *your* office?"

"My client has horse allergies. Twenty minutes—honest."

"Why did you—" the door was closing in her face, "—have a pony in your van?" she finished under her breath.

Liz entered her office slowly. The pony had upended the plant pot, and dirt littered the floor.

"Hello, baby," she approached the miniature and gently reached out to touch her curly brown back, which was barely even with her desk chair. Adjectives like "adorable" and "sweet" popped into Liz's head.

"Think what Chloe would do if she saw you!" the counselor said aloud, scratching behind the diminutive foal's ears. She sat down and listened to her messages, still eyeing her new office mate. The colt advanced guardedly, then nuzzled under Liz's arm.

"If you're looking for milk, you're out of luck," she stroked the white blaze on its nose, comforted by the feel of the soft hair. "Maybe there *is* some resemblance to a large dog," she murmured.

Two weeks earlier, the usually calm, cool, and collected Dr. Fleming tried to settle the butterflies in his stomach as he and Hope sat in the modernly adorned office of Danielle Finch, head partner at Cornerstone Associates, a premier Seattle architectural firm. Hope's face reflected a look of happy expectation, the same joyful anticipation she had worn on their way to the hospital for the birth of each child.

Danielle entered, smartly dressed and confident, a roll of papers in her hand. After greeting her new clients, she laid out the unruly pages and fastened them flat.

Hope gasped in awe. Mark fingered the edges cautiously as if afraid the print was not yet dry.

"So this is the profile of the three lots from the street," the architect began, sweeping her hand across the drawing.

Three wide and deep lots, fronting a residential street, were carved from the end of an orchard. The property's original farmhouse still stood farther up the road. The first suburb north of Seattle, this small city still had some pockets of old land holdings that were beginning to be parceled out now that the housing market was recovering.

"All three buildings will be well set back from the street. We placed the barn here," she indicated the shelter to the left. "Local ordinances will only allow you two minis per lot, so with the whole parcel you can have six. We've made the barn big enough for ten, in case you get a variance at some point. The riding corral runs across the back of the three properties."

Danielle went on to describe the office building in the middle with its therapy rooms, then the residential treatment center on the end. The construction style mimicked a farmhouse look, with large front porches and wood siding.

Mark had to fight back tears and drew several deep breaths, trying to enjoy the moment. His lifelong dream was on this table before him, and he actually had the money to accomplish it. Ever since completing his thesis on the effects of family interactions in the success or failure of adolescent psychotherapy, he had wanted to create a short-stay residential home for the youngest teens, for whom so few facilities were available at a critical juncture in their lives. For some, the stability offered by a treatment setting could make the difference in whether they recovered or not.

Mark had started reading about the success and popularity of therapeutic riding centers some years ago. Most were located far outside the city limits in rural communities. One night the idea came to him…by using miniature horses, he could create a center much closer to the city. Pre-school and younger elementary children would benefit from actually riding the horses, while the teens from the residence could be involved in the ponies' care.

He admired the individual floor plans. The residence had eight distinct bedrooms, enough for six clients and two live-in therapists. The office building had four therapy rooms, plus two playrooms and a language lab for Hope, who planned to return to her career as a speech and language specialist as soon as Junie entered kindergarten.

More pages unfolded, revealing the details of each building and the riding track. All shared a classic wood construction that would fit in with the neighborhood, should other parcels be developed into single family homes.

Danielle continued to talk about permits and restrictions, but Mark had long since stopped listening. The overall impression of the three buildings together was more than he could have ever imagined. Hope's hand found his under the table, and he knew she shared his amazement and delight.

Mark opened the middle school library door slowly, surprised by the absence of the usual tutoring students. Edwinna, seated at a long table, lost in thought and staring out the window at the gorgeous May afternoon, had not heard him enter.

Mark studied her a moment before clearing his throat. Her head turned, and he was immediately concerned. Her eyes hinted at a sadness he had not seen since the previous summer when she first came to his office.

"What's up?" He pulled out the chair opposite her.

"After-school assemblies, both schools."

"No, I mean, with you?" Down to monthly appointments, it had been several weeks since Mark had talked alone with his client.

"Not much," Edwinna continued with a forced smile. "The program got a big boost last week. We helped the high school soccer goalie raise his math grade so he didn't get benched. The team might get to State this year if we can keep his grades up. The story gave our tutoring program some good publicity. With football season in the fall, I'm expecting more athletes to come in for help."

"That's great, but I meant, something's happened with you."

"Paul's acceptance letter came from his first choice school," her voice dropped as she shuffled the papers before her. "A big, thick envelope, all about housing and freshman orientation…suddenly everything's sinking in." She gave Mark a quick glance. "These senior boys, they about make you crazy, but having them gone, out of the house, is unimaginable."

Her thoughts drifted to the nightly dinner table, with Paul, the talkative first born, cracking up his younger brother with his rendition of the day's events. Paul had the more volatile temperament, quick to heat up, quick to cool down, quick to go for the laugh. The house would be quiet without him…too quiet.

"Other mothers have described the first one leaving home as having their hearts torn out."

"That's pretty accurate." Edwinna fought back sudden tears.

They sat silently for a moment.

"It's okay to cry, you know."

Edwinna envisioned the small "Tears Welcome" sign hanging unobtrusively in Mark's office. In the early days of her sessions, her gaze had often landed on those words when she'd been desperate to look anywhere other than at her therapist.

"The day I finally got out of bed after my divorce, I vowed I'd never cry again." She pulled her hair back and raised her chin.

"And how has that worked for you?" Mark studied her face, the lines around her mouth and the beginnings of dark circles under her eyes. She had come so far from the depressed woman he had first seen in his office ten months ago; he didn't want Paul's departure to send her back to nightly wanderings. "Seems to me the last time you ignored all those emotions you ended up getting arrested with a paint brush in your hand."

"Well, that can't happen again," Edwinna smiled ruefully. "The police confiscated my best four-inch roller and a gallon of good paint, too."

"Still, why don't you humor me and come in next week? A couple extra sessions now might be a help." He pulled his calendar up on his phone. "Your regular time's available. Tuesday at five?"

Edwinna could not deny that the inward calm she had worked so hard to attain in the past year had been crumbling in bits and pieces ever since Paul's acceptance letters had started arriving.

"Okay. Tuesday at five."

Evergreen needles scratched his face as he stumbled through the woods, terrified. Home should be around the next bend in the trail, but the house never appeared. His foot slid on the muddy path and he went down on one knee, panicked that whatever was following would catch up. Struggling to stand, his muscles refused to work together.

Mark woke up frightened and disoriented, his heart pounding. Slowly, he became aware of the familiar mattress beneath him, his wife's quiet breathing, and the dim light from the bedside clock. His heartbeat slowed as he took several deep breaths, but the sweaty dampness beneath him was uncomfortable. He moved quietly into the bathroom, hanging his head over the sink and splashing cool water on his face.

Nightmares from his childhood had been showing up with alarming frequency over the past month. Mark hated the turmoil upon waking, the moment when he didn't know where he was or what had happened. When he had been young, the abrupt arousal had invariably been accompanied by wetting the bed, adding to his distress. He had learned early to wash his own sheets, and after a time his mother never inquired about his stripped bed.

He slipped back under the covers with as little movement as possible, but Hope stirred and rolled toward him.

"You okay?" she asked drowsily.

"Yes. Go back to sleep."

Her hand reached over and touched his damp t-shirt.

"Bad dream again?"

"It's okay."

She patted him with the same soft touch they used for their children's nighttime disturbances.

"I love you."

"I love you, too." Mark cupped her hand in his and soon felt her drift off.

Now came the hour of sleeplessness and increasingly anxious thoughts. How ironic that he, the consummate calm and steady counselor, was dangerously close to having nightly panic attacks. Advice offered to clients had not worked for him. Getting up to meditate rather than lying in bed worrying would only alarm Hope and start a conversation he didn't want to have in the middle of the night.

The bad dreams had re-surfaced after winning the lottery. It was not surprising that such a sudden change, even one for the better, would stir up old insecurities and unresolved feelings. But recognizing that did not diminish them.

Money had been a source of argument between his parents for as long as he could remember. His mother's tight-fisted control of the family's finances had become iron-clad when his father died during Mark's first year of college. Family support had evaporated and each of his younger siblings had been escorted to the door at age 18. Mrs. Fleming sold the family home and downsized as soon as her last child left. For some of his siblings, self-sufficiency in their thirties and forties had come only after a struggle, and Mark and Hope had supported more than one through tough times. With the lottery money, his financial worries should be over.

He remembered how happy he had been the day they first looked at the architect's plans for the treatment center. To be able to fulfill that dream now, when he was only 45, instead of having to wait until later, it was such a gift. But was it the right thing to do? Doubts started the minute they signed the first construction contracts. Should he be saving all the money instead of spending such a large chunk of it? Should he be sharing some of it with his siblings now instead of later? Or putting more in a trust for his own kids? What if the center failed and he lost everything?

"Grow up," Hope murmured suddenly as she pulled her hand out of his and rolled away from him.

"What?" Mark startled at her words.

"What?" Hope turned her head a bit, rousing.

"What did you say?" Mark whispered, staring at her profile in the dark.

"I didn't say anything," Hope replied, fully awakened now and annoyed. "Go to sleep."

"No, you said something."

Hope rolled back toward him with a sigh, again placing her hand on his chest.

"I guess I was dreaming then; I don't know. I think I was dreaming about the kids." She patted him tenderly but firmly. "Quit thinking and go to sleep."

"Okay. I just...I thought you said something."

He matched his breathing to hers, closed his eyes, and tried to empty his mind. *Things always seem worse in the middle of the night,* he lectured himself. *Breathe deeply and fully, empty your mind of everything but the breath.* The words of his meditation tape played in his mind, but Hope's "Grow up!" had disconcerted him, and he didn't know what it meant.

Edwinna drove through the dusty, dirt-packed access lane of the construction site to unload her treasures. Dr. Fleming had asked if she would like to help with the landscaping of the newly named Pony

Center as part of her community service over the summer, and she'd been delighted. While returning to weekly therapy sessions was helping ease the dread of her oldest's departure in September, planning the gardens was a welcome diversion. She was like a painter who had been handed a huge blank canvas to produce the most vibrant panorama imaginable.

Edwinna loved designing the space: privacy plantings at the fence along the back and sides of the horse track; a huge vegetable garden near the residence; butterfly-enticing plants at the corral-side entrance to the offices; and a pumpkin patch in the middle of the riding circle. At Mark's request, several apple trees remained in the northwest corner of the property as a reminder of the original orchard, and Edwinna toyed with the idea of a water feature beneath their umbrella of shade where the ponies and children could rest on warm days.

Carrying the tallest plants toward the slightly raised bed of the butterfly garden, she pushed the hair out of her eyes; the wind kept loosening short wisps which danced across her forehead. As she knocked the first plant out of its pot, unexpected shouts from above made her look up.

Flames shot from the roof of the nearly completed office building. Edwinna froze, staring in awe at the mesmerizing bright yellow trails of sparks lifting into the sky, and then the horrible realization sunk in that the wind was carrying the radiant particles to the barn where four ponies stood in their stalls.

Edwinna ran.

She dialed 9-1-1, shouting “Fire! Horses! Barn! Residence!” and the address before the dispatcher could make a single inquiry.

Hay in the front corral had caught fire and the flames were snaking into the barn. The ponies squealed and stomped as smoke swirled with the wind. Edwinna turned to see if the men on the roof could help, but they were battling the flames there. The water trough caught her eye; she pulled off her sun-protective shirt and doused it and as much of her body as she could with the water. Far-off sirens could be faintly heard; she willed them to hurry.

From the stall closest to the fire, she grabbed Oreo by his mane, covered his eyes with her shirt, and pulled him to the rear barn doors, shoving the little black and white pony into the corral. The tan and white mini, Misty, was next. As Edwinna went back for the last two ponies, a neighbor appeared.

“Grab their harnesses! By the door!” Edwinna yelled to her. The exploding fire necessitated dragging both struggling ponies together toward the back corral, where the neighbor took all-brown Clarabelle from Edwinna’s trembling grip.

The barn siding caught fire and the thick smoke choked them. Two more neighbors arrived and caught

Oreo and Misty, who were running terrified around the corral. After fumbling to get the harnesses on the uncooperative colts, all four skittering ponies were led to the relative safety of the back fence.

The group watched as two fire engines pulled up, followed by a ladder truck. The firefighters swept over the site, most heading for the fully-engaged barn.

"Are all the horses out? Anyone inside?" asked the first responder to reach the frightened group.

"Everyone's out, ponies, too." Edwinna was wheezing from the smoke. "The roofers?"

"EMTs have them." He eyed Edwinna's smudged clothing. "What about you?"

"I'll be okay." Edwinna rubbed her eyes to make the stinging stop. "I wasn't in that long."

In fact, the minutes had felt like forever. She patted trembling little Misty beside her, then followed as the group was escorted around the gushing hoses to safety across the street.

From the neighbor's fenced yard, with a tight hold on the reins of the skittish ponies, Edwinna watched in dismay as the scene unfolded before her. What just one hour ago had seemed the fulfillment of a dream was now perishing in a reeking haze of black smoke.

The barn collapsed in seeming slow motion, a fountain of sparks rising as the walls caved in and crashed to the ground. The roof of the office structure gave way suddenly and water cascaded into the building like some sort of horror-house water park ride gone wrong. And beside it, the studs of the partially-framed residence stood valiantly, despite the charring at their edges, odd black patterns decorating the soaked and dripping wood.

Amid the chaos of fire trucks, ambulances, and gawking neighbors, Edwinna observed Dr. Fleming arrive, yelling over the commotion and wildly gesturing to the first firefighter in his path. Directed across the street, relief flooded his face when he saw the huddled group, and he rushed toward them, calling the ponies by name.

The smoke, the noise, the ponies' frightened whinnying, her own thumping heart—all caught up with Edwinna like a whirlwind of vertigo. As Mark came through the gate, she released the ponies' harnesses and sank onto the porch steps, holding her head and closing her eyes. The image of the devastation in front of her seemed burned into the backs of her lids. Tears came slowly at first, but then in great, wrenching sobs.

Mark approached slowly and lowered himself beside her, the small ponies shifting in a tight group before him.

"There you go," he said quietly, attentive to his client despite the commotion surrounding them. "It's okay. Let it all come out now." He sat with her as she cried, his eyes taking in every detail of the smoldering remains.

Clarabelle nudged his arm. He reached out to her, twirling the stiff brown hair under his fingers.

One month later, Mark dropped despairingly into the chair by his colleague's office window.

"You look terrible," Liz's voice reflected her concern. In the weeks after the fire, Mark had seemed distracted but determinedly upbeat, relieved there had been no loss of life, human or equine. The rebuilding had been going well. But now he looked awful. "Are you sleeping?"

"Not really."

"Is it the fire? I thought there was insurance."

"This started before the fire. It's family."

Liz waited patiently. Their fifteen-year partnership had left few secrets between them.

"I'm getting a lot of pressure from my siblings to take in my mom."

This news was a surprise to Liz.

"But you don't get along with your mother."

"I know. It's because of the lottery. Now that we have more money, the others want Hope and me to take care of her."

"She's living alone?"

"Yup," Mark sighed. "Eighty-seven and still striking fear into every solicitor who approaches her front door."

"Could you find a nice assisted-living facility? If money isn't a problem?"

"They want her to be with family."

"Could anyone else take her?" Tales of Mrs. Fleming's explosive temper and hurtful tirades had been the topic of many conversations between them over the years.

"My brothers' wives long ago said that would never be an option for them. She's not easy to be around, you know."

"I do recall you've mentioned that. Several hundred times, I think. Could you hire in some help? Overnight or for a block of time during the day?"

"She won't have strangers in the house."

"I don't suppose she has any living siblings you could bunk her with?"

"None of them want her, either."

"Do you realize you are throwing up roadblocks to every possible solution?" Exasperation seeped into Liz's usually well-modulated voice.

Mark shrugged.

"Here," Liz stood and shoved her swivel chair until it was directly across from him, "put your roadblocks and negativities in the chair and talk to them."

The consummate counselor smiled wearily. "Very funny."

"I'm serious. Good for the goose, good for the gander. Physician heal thyself. Can't hurt, might help. All that stuff. Talk to the chair."

"All right." Although worn out, Mark felt the need to prove the therapy technique was, in fact, helpful. He cleared his throat to begin and directed his remarks to the empty chair. "Why are you being so negative to every idea that's presented? I need to find a solution. I need positive help, not negativity." He got up and sat in Liz's chair and thought for a moment before responding as his negative self.

"Because you aren't listening. What is the real issue here? Why are you even thinking about something that you know will be a disaster? You've never gotten along well with your mother; she's difficult, controlling, opinionated, and brings her daughters-in-law to tears every time…still. Living with you is simply not an option. You are being unrealistic if you think it is."

Mark returned to his original place.

"Well, she's mellowed a little. And Hope has always gotten along with her the best of anyone in the family. It might work. We could hire help at home."

Switch.

"Just because Hope can get along with her for an hour at a time, doesn't mean it will work out 24/7. Do you want to ruin the most important relationship in your life?"

Switch.

"But I'm not seeing any other solutions. The others think I have to do this, it's my responsibility as the oldest, especially now that we have more money."

Switch.

"Then give the money to your brothers and let them deal with her," Mark's negative self replied sarcastically.

Switch.

"That would never work."

Mark stayed in his chair and simply turned his head to indicate he now represented his roadblocks again.

"Then how could it possibly work for you and Hope to take her? What miraculous capabilities do you two have that would make that happen? Infinite patience? Impermeably thick skin? Young children who won't be affected by scathing criticism?"

Kindhearted and idealistic, Mark rallied to his mother's defense.

"She's actually quite good with the kids, I'll give her that. They love her. She holds her tongue around them."

"This is all about guilt. You are feeling guilty because of the lottery money," the negatives attacked again.

Mark didn't have another comeback and sighed dejectedly.

Liz slipped into her chair and put her hand on her friend's arm.

"Give it a little while, Mark. Leave all your options open, don't make any commitments until you've really thought it over and talked to Hope. A lot."

The sound of heels clicking down the hallway indicated that Mark's session had ended. Liz ducked into his office. Absorbed in finishing up his written notes, he startled when she plopped down in the straight-backed chair near his desk.

"I have an idea," her voice trembled with excitement. "SUCH a good idea."

"Yes?" Half-listening, he had been in the middle of a thought and was trying to remember the end of his sentence.

"No, I really have a great idea. And I want you to park all your roadblocks somewhere else and think about it. Okay?"

"I'm listening."

"What if…just hear me out…what if you added a master bedroom, a little living room, and a private bath to the residence at the Pony Center, and moved your mother in there?"

"With my troubled young teens."

"You said she got along with kids. That's what gave me the idea. I bet she'd have a lot to contribute."

"But she can't take care of herself much longer."

"Then include a bedroom for a caregiver."

"A caregiver just for her?"

"What if it was part-time for her and part-time for the ponies?"

"That doesn't make sense."

"Think about it. And I might have the person for you."

"Who?"

"My sister."

Mark looked at the hope in Liz's eyes. No wonder she was so excited about the idea.

"Your sister, the felon," he deadpanned.

"Well, there's that, yes. But she'd be great with the ponies, and I'm sure she could learn to be a good caregiver. The experience might open some other work possibilities for her in the future. Her record may be expunged after five years; the attorney's working on that as part of the plea."

"So now I've got a felon and my cranky mother around traumatized, emotionally disturbed children in treatment."

"Sounds like a real family to me."

A real family.

The words reverberated in Mark's head. Liz might have a point. Maybe. It just might work.

Chapter Eight: Roberta and the Twins

March—October, 2012

"Mom," Frannie began, "we have something to tell you."

This was never a good beginning. Whenever both twins had something to tell their mother together, it was usually not good news.

Previous confessions had included:

"We skipped school and got caught."

"We had an accident in the car." (One was driving but the other was navigating badly.)

"We don't know what to do with our lives after college."

And, finally, last May, "We want to move back home."

As her twin daughters stood before her bursting with news, Roberta steeled herself and sank into a kitchen chair.

"It's good news," said Gwen, twin two. "Really."

"Okay. I'm listening."

"This might seem sort of sudden, but—"

"We're in love! We want to get married!" Frannie, twin one, finished her sister's sentence enthusiastically.

A glaze crossed Roberta's eyes. "Excuse me?"

"You know those boys we've been dating? The nice ones?" Gwen reclaimed the conversation with a take-it-slowly warning look to her sister.

"The ones who are roommates and I've never met. In the eight months you've lived at home, they've never crossed the threshold even once—those 'nice' boys?"

"There's a reason for that. We thought you might not like them," Frannie said.

"Oh?"

"Not that there's a *logical* reason for you not to like them. Not at all." Gwen.

"But you and Dad can be weird about things sometimes." Frannie.

"Well, what is it? I'm a reasonable person." Roberta looked from one twin to the other expectantly. "Different race? Different religion? Tattoos?"

"Well—" Gwen.

"They're twins," Frannie blurted.

"What?"

"They're twins, too. Twins, also, I mean." Gwen.

"Twins?"

"Identical. Isn't that something?" Frannie, with a forced smile.

"Identical?"

"You know, but just like with the Dents, we can tell them apart. Allen has a little scar at his hairline from hitting the soccer goal post in high school." Gwen, proudly. "He was the keeper."

"And Brett broke his fingers playing baseball. He's the catcher. The knuckles on his left hand are a little weird. We call them 'A' and 'B.' Isn't that cute?" Frannie's smile faded at her mother's unrelenting consternation.

"Mom? Do you want us to start over?" Gwen.

"NO! No, just keep going. All of a sudden you want to get married?"

"Not all of a sudden. We've known for months, but we were afraid to tell you. They haven't told their parents, either."

"Two weddings? How soon?"

"No, that's the best part!" Frannie.

"We'll have a double wedding!" Gwen and Frannie together.

Roberta's brain flared to life again with volcanic fervor. "No! Absolutely not. You each need to have your own special day. A double wedding with twins times two? It would be like a bad Disney movie—*Parent Trap Grows Up*."

The girls launched into what was obviously a pre-rehearsed litany:

"But, Mom, listen. A double wedding's so much easier. We'd be inviting all the same family members, why make everyone travel for two different dates?"

"And which of us would go first? No one would want to come back again the next weekend or month for the other wedding."

"And who would get the best weather weekend of the year?"

"And why have double the expense when you can feed everyone one time? On *both* sides? The only difference will be some of our friends. It might be a little bigger than either of us would have had alone, but it'll cost way less than two separate weddings."

"What did your father say?"

"We haven't told him yet," Gwen nervously shifted from one foot to the other.

"We wanted to tell you first. In case, you know, we need some help with him," Frannie added. "You know how he can be about things. Dating kinds of things."

Roberta looked into the bright, eager faces of her firstborns, recognizing that she was, once again, as she had seemingly been *forever*, hopelessly and utterly double-teamed.

The first Saturday in August dawned with a perfect blue sky and the promise of temperatures in the mid-seventies. Tony's phone buzzed at 10:30 a.m. while he sipped a second cup of coffee and perused his favorite internet intelligence websites. He was surprised to see Roberta's name pop up, remembering (from happier days) that today was the big day in the Lovell household. Donna should be delivering flowers for the afternoon wedding in just a few hours.

"Good morning, Roberta. What's up?"

"Tony, thank God you picked up! The boys are missing."

"What boys?"

"Allen and Brett, the grooms!" Roberta's voice was taut. "They went out for their bachelor party last night and never came back. They were supposed to be at a wedding breakfast with their parents and relatives at ten o'clock and never showed up. The girls are hysterical."

"They're probably sleeping off their hangovers. Where did they go and who were they with?"

"Their frat brothers took them out."

Tony's response level raised a notch as he considered all the frat-brother-drinking horror stories he knew.

"Their parents started trying to reach them at 9:30. They've already checked the apartment; there's no sign the boys returned last night. Adelle and Bob are calling the hospitals, and they tried to put in a police report. That didn't get very far, because, you know, they're only half-an-hour overdue."

"Where was the bachelor party?"

"The girls don't know. It was a big secret, a surprise. A double surprise because of the circumstances. Tony," Roberta's voice dropped low, "I've got a house full of relatives and 400 people coming to the church at four o'clock this afternoon. You *have* to help me."

"Of course. Put one of the girls on the phone."

"I don't think they can talk." Distinct weeping could be heard in the background.

"Okay, put your phone on speaker. What's the name of the fraternity?"

The twins, sitting miserably at the kitchen table, did their best to provide information between tearful sobs. They came up with the names of the two best men, four ushers, and a few other frat brothers they thought might be with their fiancés.

"Who do you think the one in charge might have been?" Tony already had the fraternity's website for the previous year pulled up on his computer. "How about Stephen? Or Mario?"

"No," the girls replied.

"What about…" He looked down the list and found the social coordinator. "How about Les?"

"Yes, he might have been. And he's Brett's best man."

"Okay, Roberta, get off speaker for a minute."

"I'm here."

"I'll be there in about twenty minutes. Have the girls make me a list with as much information as possible about each of those names, especially Les and the other best man. In particular, if they could get birthdates, that would help."

"Birthdates?"

"I'm hoping I can trace some credit card transactions. I'm assuming the grooms wouldn't be paying."

"Wait, I'm trying to write this down."

"And, make sure one of the girls keeps her cell phone open at all times. Call the boys' folks and tell them the same thing, keep one line open at all times. I'm sure the guys will call someone as soon as they realize the time."

"Okay. We'll do that." Roberta felt a little less desperate.

"One more thing. Were any of those boys in any military program, flight school, anything like that?"

"Flight? Do you think they've flown somewhere?" The panic in her voice returned.

"Probably not, never mind. I'll see you in twenty. Wait, what time did they leave last night?"

"Girls, what time did they leave?"

"Five o'clock."

Tony figured the time in his head: Left at 5 p.m., had to be back by, say 9:00 a.m. in time to clean up for the breakfast. That left sixteen hours. Two hours transportation each way seemed like the maximum a group would travel for a drinking night. So they couldn't be that far away. Unless they'd flown. But where would they go? Vegas was too far for an overnight. And a big group would be difficult and expensive to transport by air. It made more sense that they would be in vehicles. Most likely the whole crew was at one of the northern casinos where they'd lost track of time. Or, they were somewhere with bad cell reception, which could be a pretty big area. If he could get their credit card information, he'd find them soon enough.

Once at Roberta's house, it took Tony less than an hour before he had the manager of the Black Bear Casino on the line and ready to enter hotel rooms 340, 341, and 342. While "missing grooms," and "hysterical brides" had gotten him no help, "big law suit if these boys are dead from drinking in your hotel" did catch the manager's attention. Within minutes a sleepy, bewildered voice replaced that of the manager on the phone.

Roberta, her husband Hal, and the girls sat watching Tony's face as he conducted his interrogation, apparently interrupted twice when the kid had to go throw up.

"Keep your phone on, wake the others up, and get dressed," Tony's last words were stern. "Stay there until the police contact you. You were the last people to see Allen and Brett, so you'll each have to give a statement." He turned to the anxious group. "Bad news first: Allen, Brett, the two best men, and four ushers are not with the fifteen hung over kids at the casino at the moment. Sometime in the early morning, they went on to another unknown location for the last surprise." The girls began to cry again.

"The good news is, neither of the grooms was drinking heavily, and most likely one of them was staying sober enough to drive. This kid was not exactly sure which twin was which. But they're in a black Suburban rented from the university district, so I'll have that plate number shortly."

"What was the last surprise?" Frannie asked.

"These boys didn't know. But your guys all had their clothes for this morning's brunch with them. So apparently, they thought they were going straight there. They're probably not too far away, and it's excellent news that the grooms were sober, or close to it. We'll find them. Now I need all the info on those best men and ushers. Can we get parent names and phone numbers, find out who might have a cabin, a plane, a boat, anything like that?"

"A boat or a plane?" Gwen repeated.

"Maybe a grand entrance was part of the scheme. The brunch was on the waterfront, you said? Maybe they were going to arrive in style…float plane or boat. I think we can take hot air balloons off the table."

"Les does like to do things in a big way." Frannie wiped her eyes for the hundredth time.

In another half hour, Tony had discovered the reservations made by Allen's best man for a cruise boat leaving at 6 a.m. from a city pier. A check with the proprietor showed the boys had never arrived.

"Okay, now we've narrowed it down to someplace between the casino and the dock. Someplace they would have no cell service. They might have left in the dark, but it would have been daylight by five a.m.; any accident just off the road should have been visible. I'm going out front to call a friend and look at a map." Tony headed for the porch, grabbing a donut from a tray on the counter along the way.

Roberta sat down beside Frannie and hugged her.

"They don't drink that much, Mom."

"I know."

"They must have had an accident. What could have happened to all eight of them?"

"I don't know. Look, you two have to stop crying." Roberta gave Gwen a reassuring hug, too. "Let's get cold cloths on your faces."

"We're supposed to get our hair done in less than an hour." This started a new round of tears.

"We'll call the shop and explain. There's still plenty of time. And you two know how to do your own hair. You can send your sisters and the other bridesmaids and you two stay home if we're still waiting."

"But what if—" for once neither twin could complete the sentence.

"I don't know. We just have to wait. I'll call Adelle and tell her what we've learned so far."

Tony spent twenty minutes on the phone with various law enforcement friends, ending with the County Sheriff's Search and Rescue Division.

"Look at Map 7." Tony overlaid maps on his computer, trying to pinpoint places without cell phone reception between the casino and the downtown dock. "What if they came out of the casino, got turned around, and headed north on the freeway? Maybe they drove for fifteen minutes, realized their mistake, and got off at the next exit. That's 220. But they didn't see it was an exit only, and they couldn't get back on the freeway going south. So now they were either still trying to go north to find something with a southbound on-ramp, or they went south on back roads trying to find Entrance 216. If they went south on the west side back roads, there are all sorts of places they could get lost. Could you put up the helicopter to look?"

Tony returned to the kitchen, snagging another donut.

"I think maybe they got disoriented around the casino and are lost. Just not that many other places without cell reception within a two-hour radius of here. And out of eight guys, surely one of them would have called if he could. A helicopter will be in the air in about twenty minutes. They'll find them if they're off the road somewhere."

"Brett promised me he'd keep his phone on," Gwen said.

"That's good to know. Nothing's shown up so far when my buddy tried to get a signal from any of those numbers."

When her brother arrived from the hotel with sandwiches, snacks, and fruit, Roberta busied herself making coffee and tea and looking after her houseguests. But the minutes dragged on and she thought she'd jump out of her skin if they didn't get news soon. Tony looked at his watch every ten minutes as he imagined the flight of the helicopter and how long it would take to travel forty miles from the north end sheriff's station to the area around the casino.

At 1:42:56 on Tony's watch, his phone sounded, startling everyone in the kitchen. Roberta sent up a solemn prayer promising nearly anything if everyone could be okay. All eyes were on Tony's face as he jotted notes after his initial thumbs up signal.

"All right, thanks," Tony smiled reassuringly at the group. "Everyone's okay." The twins burst into tears simultaneously. "The Suburban went 150 feet backwards down a steep embankment out of sight of the road when Brett was making a K-turn to get turned around. It rolled twice. Les tried to climb out of the ravine, fell, and has what the EMTs think is either a broken ankle or a bad sprain. He'll be headed for the hospital along with the two ushers who were in the center seats and only had lap belts. They'll be checked for internal injuries. Everyone else is just a little banged up. Brett's in good shape with no alcohol or drug impairment according to the responders. Allen might have a black eye where he hit the side window. Ironically, the alcohol in the others probably kept them relaxed and helped prevent anything more serious." He glanced at his watch. "They ought to be back in cell range just about—"

Both girls' phones went off instantaneously, and they raced to opposite corners of the kitchen.

"I'll call Bob," Hal headed to a separate room for a conversation with the boys' father.

Roberta sent up a silent prayer of thanks and vowed to keep all her previous, desperate promises, especially the ones regarding Tony.

"How can I ever thank you? I don't know what we would have done."

"Well," Tony took one more donut from the plate, "actually, there is one thing you could do for me."

"Anything. You name it."

"I'm in some trouble with Donna. Maybe you could put in a good word for me. Will you see her at the church when she brings the flowers?"

"Of course! I didn't realize you two were seeing each other."

"It was going real well until I did something stupid. I'm hoping I still have a chance with her. Maybe you could mention that I was helpful to you. *Electronically* helpful. If you want to say I *saved the day*, that would be even better," he urged hopefully.

Roberta laughed. “How bad is it?”

“She’s pretty pissed. Found out I interfered a little in her divorce. Remember what a wreck she was last May? With her husband dragging it out and making her miserable? I helped things along a bit.”

“A bit?”

“Quite a bit. Nothing illegal. I encouraged him to settle up fairly and quickly, that’s all.”

“I see. *‘Fairly and quickly.’* I don’t even want to know how you managed that. How did Donna find out?”

“The girlfriend. One night, Taffy and Judd were having a drunken pity party with themselves because their standard of living had taken a nosedive once the assets had to be divided more evenly. Judd mentioned something about being blackmailed before he passed out, so Taffy called up Donna to complain. It didn’t take long for Donna to put it together with me. Then, suddenly, I’m in the doghouse. Me, who didn’t do anything. Well, hardly anything.”

Roberta observed Tony thoughtfully. *Who are you?* More than a year after she had first met him, she still didn’t have a clue.

When Roberta finally arrived at the church with the twins (her husband Hal was bringing the Dents, the other girls, and their dresses straight from the hair salon), Donna met her at the door.

"I was getting so worried!" Donna led the way to the changing room, a dress bag billowing from one hand. Outside the commandeered Sunday School room, bouquets, corsages, and boutonnières lay ready on a table. Hearing from Roberta at two o'clock that everything was running late, Donna had decided to stay to lend a hand pinning on the flowers. Trying to jab a three-inch stick pin into expensive clothing could be a bit daunting for the uninitiated—even on a good day.

"I can't even begin to tell you…." Roberta hung Gwen's dress on a wall hook.

Commotion and deep voices announced the arrival of the boys. Donna peeked out the door and was shocked to see a large entourage surrounding the male side of the wedding party: two young men who would have been identical except one was holding ice to his bruised face, another young man scratched up and on crutches, two fellows with facial discolorations, and two more walking gingerly. Parents were hovering, carrying tuxes and shoes, while another group of friends languished at the end of the hall, apparently forbidden to proceed further.

"What on earth happened?" Donna turned to Roberta.

"The wedding party got lost in the middle of the night up west of the casinos. Brett was trying to turn a rented Suburban around on a narrow road and backed down a 150-foot cliff. They rolled it twice. Then Les, that's Brett's best man, tried to climb out of the ravine and fell, breaking his ankle. They were out of cell phone range, of course. We're lucky they weren't all killed."

"Oh, my, how did you ever find them?"

"I called Tony." Roberta glanced at Donna to see how this news would be taken, but there was no reaction on Donna's part. "I saw him last fall when Liz's niece went missing, and his name popped into my head as the person who could help." Packing up the empty dress bag, Roberta looked at Donna earnestly. "He was wonderful, Donna. He absolutely saved the day. I don't know what we would have done without him."

Donna busied herself pulling out the other silk organza gown as if she hadn't heard. "Should I be careful not to mix these dresses up?"

"No, we can tell them apart. Anyway, Tony said I should mention to you that he was extremely helpful, 'electronically' helpful. Honestly, we were in a panic. The boys' parents had checked the hospitals and the police couldn't help. Tony came over, got some information from the girls, tracked the two best men's credit cards, and then got the sheriff to send up a helicopter when he had a pretty good idea where they might be. He was truly heroic."

"I thought so, too, at one time," Donna finally responded. She flashed back to November, being trapped under the tree, and to how glad she had been to see Tony as he forced his way through the debris. "But he's not to be trusted." She shook off the memory. "Do you know he has vehicles hidden in garages all over the north end?"

"Hidden? Or parked?"

"And that computer nearly chained to his wrist. It gets a little old." Donna's eyes welled with tears. In the two-and-a-half months since she had ended their relationship, she had talked to no one about Tony, not even Liz. As much as she loved her counselor, she couldn't trust her to be completely objective about Tony.

The younger twins and other bridesmaids arrived from the hair salon and the noise level in the room went exponential. Roberta signaled Donna to come out to the hall while the girls touched up their make-up before dressing.

"So what happened with you two?" Roberta asked.

"He interfered in my divorce," Donna replied quietly. "Last October, Judd unexpectedly settled very favorably. I didn't understand why he had a change of heart, but who looks a gift horse in the mouth? I was just so happy to be finished with it."

"And?"

"Tony had been digging around and found some other affairs Judd had, as well as one slight business impropriety at the nursery. He threatened to tell me and the kids if Judd didn't stop dragging his feet in the divorce."

"And what is your problem with having some help to get out of what was a terrible time for you…if you remember those days of endless sobbing?"

"He was dishonest about it."

"Dishonest? He lied about his involvement?"

"Dishonest by omission, then. He was secretive. He's *always* secretive."

"Secretive or private?" Roberta prodded gently.

"Let's not talk about it now." Donna felt her anger rise. "I want to enjoy this day with you, your gorgeous daughters, and their slightly banged up grooms."

"Okay, but we'll talk later, all right?"

"Sometime, I promise." With that, Donna answered the call to help with boutonnières.

An hour later, standing at the back of the church, Donna watched the brides go down the aisle, one on each side of Hal, followed by their identical twin sisters walking together, and then the rest of the bridesmaids. The flowers, the bridal gowns, the dresses, the boy's shirts…all the colors went together perfectly. Roberta stood beaming at the front of the packed church.

Donna sighed. In the early spring, she had finally been feeling some happiness, only to be completely blindsided by Tony's betrayal. And she wasn't too pleased with her counselor, either, even though Liz claimed Tony had misunderstood her directive to wait until the divorce was settled before attempting a relationship.

Donna's hip vibrated. Rather, her phone was vibrating in her pants pocket. A text message. From Liz. Odd, Donna thought. Liz had only rarely called to change an appointment time, and had certainly never texted previously. Surely she knew this afternoon was the wedding.

Donna slipped into the back stairwell and checked the message: "Tony at hosp heart attack serious call me"

Donna read the message three times. A heart attack? How was that possible? He had been helping Roberta only that morning. Donna went down the stairs to the social hall beneath the church's sanctuary and returned the call.

"Oh, Donna, I'm glad you got my message. Has the wedding started?"

"They just went down the aisle. What happened with Tony?"

"I'm not sure, someone called me from the ambulance. They were out in the county doing a search for a toddler who wandered away from a campsite. He developed chest pains and collapsed. Luckily, there were EMTs on the scene already, so he got treatment fast."

"Why call me? We're not seeing each other anymore."

"I realize that, but I thought you'd want to know. He's been morose ever since you broke up."

"Which hospital?"

"University."

"Why did they call you?"

"I'm listed as the emergency contact on his phone. He doesn't have any family out here."

Donna's silence expressed more than she was able to put into words. Finally, her thoughts coalesced.

"I'll try to drop by after the ceremony. But no promises. About anything."

"Thank you," Liz sighed. "I'll see you there."

Five days later, Donna carted Tony's small overnight suitcase from her car up to the front door of his modest home. Although they had dated almost five months, she'd never been inside his house. Walking gingerly, Tony followed. The emergency double by-pass had taken more out of him than he'd expected, either from the surgery itself or the alarming comeuppance that he was no longer an invincible, if slightly pudgy, former Marine.

"I'll carry that," he protested.

"Nothing over ten pounds for six weeks, you know what the doctor said."

Donna opened the door, half expecting to walk into an electronic maze worthy of a cold war spy movie. She was almost disappointed when she saw a normal-looking home.

"I'll take your things to the bedroom," she said, finding her way down the hall. She glanced into the first room she passed, anticipating a center for covert surveillance, but it was only a den with an outdated box television and a wall of books. Tony's bedroom was next. He followed her and headed for the bathroom.

The room was neat and tidy, but not obsessively so. A small group of pictures accented one corner of his dresser: two young attractive brunettes, circa 1970 or '80 by their hairstyles; a large group picture of what must be his family at a wedding; and a small frame with a mother holding a newborn. Donna picked up the last photo and examined it closely: It wasn't the common image of a knit-capped baby, snugly wrapped in its mother's arms on the hospital bed. The mother was in regular clothing and the background held cots and tables as if it were a shelter of some sort.

Donna's eyes went back to the portraits of the two dark-haired beauties.

"Who are these women?" she called into the bathroom.

"My ex-wives." A second later, the toilet flushed.

"You still have pictures of your ex-wives? Haven't you been single for over twenty-some years now? Do you still love them?"

Tony came out of the bathroom, wiping his hands on a towel. Interestingly, his face had taken on a more healthy color since his surgery. Donna had perhaps mistaken his previous paleness as the absence of Seattle sunshine rather than impaired circulation.

"They divorced me, you know. My loving them was never the question. My love of alcohol was the problem. Before I met you, I did miss them. A lot."

"What about this one?" Donna held up the picture of the infant.

"That's the second baby I delivered. He was born in a shelter in New Orleans during Katrina."

"You were there?"

"My Search and Rescue team arrived in the worst of it. We found a mother in labor and got her to a shelter. She'd been in her attic all night with just her five-year-old. Her husband left to get help and never made it back. It took…" he could see the blue color of the baby with the cord wrapped around its neck, "it took some effort to get that baby breathing, but it was okay. The parents got reunited a couple days later, and she sent me the picture. I wanted to stay in touch, but I think they probably moved. I only heard from her the one time."

"So where was the first baby?"

"Sarajevo, in a hospital we were trying to evacuate. This mom was delivering. That time I pretty much just caught the kid, didn't really know what I was doing. It was thrilling and frightening at the same time. After that, I read up about childbirth and made sure I had some gear in my emergency duffels." Tony slowly sank onto the edge of his bed, strangely tired. He studied Donna's back as she examined the other details of his room. Her eyes finally came around and rested on him.

"It was wrong, you know."

"*I know*, I know. I thought I was doing the right thing, but it was selfish of me. I wanted you to be free so we could be together. But I was wrong." Tony stared at the floor before lifting his eyes to meet hers. "I shouldn't have rushed things. I know that now. It had been so long since I'd met anyone who made me feel happy, I didn't want to take a chance on losing that."

"So where's your magical seat of operations? Where's all the spy stuff?"

"Nothing like that. All I've got is my computer. And my phone."

"Do you have a file on me?"

"Of course not."

"I don't believe you. What's on your computer?"

"Nothing." That was the truth, now.

"Let me see Judd's file."

"I destroyed it. It was never meant for you to see. It was just a threat."

Donna studied him. When she'd arrived at the hospital on the day of his collapse, he had looked so bad most of the anger had drained right out of her. Over the next four days, he had been extremely weak and unlike himself. It was like starting the relationship all over again. Now she looked at him critically and tried to decide: Could she trust him or not?

"You'd be perfectly justified to never forgive me," Tony said contritely. "But I am truly, truly sorry that I hurt you. And if you give me another chance, I…."

Donna dropped gently onto the bed beside him. Tony placed his arm tentatively around her shoulder.

"I've missed you so much," he said softly.

"I've missed you, too." She gave a long sigh but still held herself apart. "You made me *so* angry. I felt betrayed just like Judd all over again."

"I know that now. I never meant to hurt you, Donna. I love you."

Donna settled against him a little bit and was quiet before speaking again.

"I guess any relationship is bound to have a rough patch or two. Especially with as much baggage as we've got." She looked at him intently. "But you have to absolutely promise me you'll never interfere behind my back again."

Tony answered by kissing her, and as her arms lightly encircled him, it seemed the most tender, loving, and exquisite embrace in his entire life.

Roberta sat across from Liz in mid-August, tanned, relaxed, and enjoying the absence of the ten pounds she'd managed to lose before the weddings, a happy smile on her face.

"So the brides have moved out, and you're down to the other two. When do they go back to school?"

"Ten days."

"And you're ready for that? Ready for the empty nest this time?"

"I am."

"Tell me."

"Two major changes. I'm going to facilitate a support group at work for cancer patients and their caregivers—one night a week."

"That's a great idea. I can tell already you have much more energy compared to last year at this time."

"The second thing is, Hal and I have committed to one trek each weekend, either biking or hiking. We're going to attempt to keep up our exercise, weather permitting. And then we'll go to a movie. We're reinstating date night."

"Wonderful!"

"I'm ready this time. I really am."

Three weeks later, Roberta was checking a billing question in the back office of the clinic when she heard a commotion and a raised voice at the front desk. Sticking her head around the corner she observed an elderly woman dressed in a fur coat (despite the September heat wave) and a wide-brimmed, bright red hat, rapping the hook of her cane sharply on the high counter.

"I have an appointment, and I need to see the doctor *immediately*."

"I'm terribly sorry, but your appointment isn't until Friday," the receptionist, Nadeen, responded politely.

"My acid reflux is very uncomfortable and my medication isn't working. I want to see the doctor right away. *Who's in charge?*"

Roberta slipped behind the counter with a welcoming smile. "I'm Roberta, the office manager. How may I help you?"

"She's got the wrong day," Nadeen whispered, pointing to the schedule on the computer screen. "New patient."

The heavy cane rapped loudly on the counter again.

"I need to see the doctor!"

The outside clinic door opened and a woman hurried in, a large bag over one shoulder and a manila folder under her arm.

"Mrs. Fleming!" The newcomer addressed the elderly woman causing the next strike of the cane on the counter to halt in mid-air. "Here are the papers."

Roberta stared at her. She seemed familiar in some way.

"Papers?" Mrs. Fleming turned to the younger woman, whose hair was just beginning to show flecks of gray.

"Here." The companion placed the pages in Roberta's outstretched hand. "We stopped by to drop off these new patient information forms before Mrs. Fleming's visit on Friday."

"Friday?" Mrs. Fleming looked momentarily confused.

"Yes, remember? You wanted to be sure the papers got here in time. That's why we came." She turned to Roberta. "I'm sorry, I guess I shouldn't have let her come in alone, but the lot is pretty full so I dropped her at the door and then parked the car."

Roberta glanced down at the top form. Under next of kin, *Mark Fleming, Ph.D.,* was written in a meticulous, if shaky hand.

"Your son is Dr. Fleming?" Roberta asked the new patient.

"Yes," she replied proudly. "And I'm living in his new home."

"The Pony Center up the street," the caregiver clarified quietly.

"And you are?" Roberta asked.

"Ginger Brubaker, her assistant," nodding toward the older woman with a smile.

The way the corners of her mouth turned and her eyes lit up made Roberta realize why she looked familiar. That was Liz's smile.

"Is anyone going to get me in to see the doctor?" Mrs. Fleming interrupted.

"Not today. On Friday," Ginger reminded her. "We're going home now." She turned to Roberta. "We'll come again on Friday."

"No problem. So you're staying in the new residence up there?"

"I started two weeks ago. I'm taking care of the ponies until Dr. Fleming gets it all organized with the residential kids doing the work. The rest of the time, I take care of Mrs. Fleming. Though she's quite—"

"Why are we still standing here?" Mrs. Fleming banged her cane on the floor.

"We're leaving right now, and we'll be back on Friday." Ginger took her arm and guided her gently toward the door.

On a whim, Roberta turned left out of the parking lot after work and drove the mile up to the Pony Center. She had not gone past it since right after the fire. Now she parked at one end of the block and walked over to the fence. The well-worn path through the tall grass plantings indicated that neighborhood children had found the same vantage point. The ponies were being walked, each carrying a small child. Mrs. Fleming, still in her fur coat and red hat, kept pace alongside the black horse, deep in conversation with the handler.

As Roberta watched, Dr. Fleming appeared on the back porch of the middle building and walked to the corral fence.

"Dr. Mark!" excited calls came from several children.

"Hey, Gordon! Hi, Chloe! You guys are looking good!"

Roberta scrutinized the children more carefully as they came past her the next time. Although it had been almost a year since she had glimpsed Chloe on the beach that day with Poochie, and the riding helmet shielded her hair, the little girl in the purple shirt was surely Liz's niece.

Roberta felt the sun's warmth through her clothes. She stood perfectly still, having an at-one-with-the-universe moment, enjoying the sound of the horses plodding in the dirt, the sensation of the light breeze on her face, and the awareness of her own peaceful breath. The Dents had been gone for eleven days. Hal was working late, there was no hurry to get home to the empty house. Relaxed and content, she simply enjoyed watching the stocky little ponies walk steadily around the ring, carrying their small charges with seemingly good-natured patience.

Head down, Roberta turned the hallway corner and approached the counseling offices. Dr. Fleming leaned against the wall, phone to his ear, and Roberta turned her head discreetly so he couldn't see her tear-streaked face.

"Yes, Mom, it's okay," he was saying into his cell phone. "The kids are allowed to be out with the ponies. That's the whole idea, remember? It's therapy for them. Yes, you can go out there, too."

Even the vision of the fur-draped, cane-wielding Mrs. Fleming amongst the horses couldn't lighten Roberta's mood. Thankfully, Liz was just approaching the waiting room and waved her back to the office.

Roberta slumped onto the couch and burst into tears.

"What is it?" a shocked Liz responded. In the three years she had been counseling Roberta intermittently, she had never seen her in such distress. A month ago, she had seemed happy and well-prepared for the next chapter of her life. "What's happened?"

"Eighteen days," Roberta sobbed. "I've had exactly 18 days of empty nest."

"But I thought you were doing so well with it." The confusion in Liz's voice made it plain she didn't understand. "The twins both making new homes with their husbands, and the other girls headed back to school. You seemed prepared for the change."

Roberta sniffled and reached for the tissue box.

"I *was*. It was…freeing. The other day I ran naked from our shower to the laundry room for a clean towel, not worrying about who might be coming in the front door with friends at any moment. There's privacy. And other things. The fridge stays full. There's no wet laundry hanging everywhere because they're afraid their clothes will shrink in the dryer. And the gas gauge needle in my car has barely moved off 'Full!'" Tears cascaded down her cheeks.

"Then what's wrong? I'm missing something."

"Dent Two—Kelsey—called last night." She yanked another tissue from the box with frustration. "She'd gotten a ride home with a friend and was standing outside the front door. She didn't want to scare us by using her key. She wants to leave school and move home."

"Oh, no."

"She's miserable. She was miserable last year, too. Quite honestly, with the weddings, we really didn't address her concerns over the summer the way we should have. I thought it was the bad roommates, first the alcoholic and then the recluse," Roberta paused, remembering with sadness her daughter's bad luck in the freshman dorm.

"I don't know if we should make her go back or let her quit. She's the quietest of the four girls, always has lived in the shadow of the others." Roberta took a discouraged swipe at the tears on her cheeks and sighed.

This parenting thing was making her crazy. "It might be good for her to come home and be the only one for a change."

"I'm so sorry," Liz sympathized compassionately. "But even if she moves home, it doesn't have to change the new things you're doing—the support group, your goal for weekend adventures with Hal."

"I know, I know." Roberta sighed before murmuring quietly, "But, I liked it. I liked running naked through the house."

Liz burst out laughing. "I'm sorry—the visual popped into my head. Hal would probably like it, too. Maybe you could take Kelsey's key so she always has to ring the bell?"

"Maybe." Roberta quieted a bit as if replaying the evening in her head. "Oh, yeah," she added absent-mindedly. "One more thing, and you'll love this part. Kelsey arrived with a puppy under her arm."

"A puppy?"

"Found it last week. I think it was the final kick to send her home. Someone giving away puppies at the store, it was the last one. She couldn't keep it at school, of course." Roberta's tone held a fatalistic irony.

"How do you feel about that?"

"Honestly? I don't mind. He'll be company for our dog. He's a pretty cute little mutt."

"I suppose coming home with a dog is better than coming home with a real baby. Especially in a family prone to twins."

"True."

Liz was talking about stress relievers, but Roberta's attention wandered. She gazed out the window. Fall would turn to winter. The winds and rains would pick up, the holidays would come and go, and then, just when the January darkness made you so low you couldn't stand it, the first crocuses would poke up with the promise of spring. A wet, gray spring, of course, but the bulbs would be testament of another winter survived.

She thought of her identical daughters, Jessica and Kelsey, mirror images of each other since conception. Perhaps it *was* time, after 19 years, to separate them. Somehow, in her mind, they had been like exquisite tulips standing tall beside each other, but with their bulbs still fused because she had been too tired to dig them up and divide them. She had thought their strength was in being together. But perhaps there was more to it than that.

Maybe it was time to step up and be the parent she was meant to be, to help them exist apart and flourish. She could do that, she told herself. She really could.

"Are you okay?" Observing her client lost in thought, Liz had been patiently waiting before resuming.

"I guess I am," Roberta answered. "I think I'm okay."

Acknowledgments

I would like to thank my husband Richard, children Katie, Roxanne and Brian, and sons-in-law Matt and Matt, for their support during the writing of this novel. Their ideas, proofreading, computer aid and general helpfulness were invaluable.

I would like to thank all my friends, and especially: Betsy, for teaching me the concept of forging ahead and creating a body of work; the Faith Lutheran Church Women's Book Group, who have discussed what makes a "good read" for over twenty-five years; Nancy and crew, for cooking community dinners; Pam's church and others, for hosting said dinners; Kathy, who never minds reading a first draft; all the twins I have known; my novel writing workshop peers; and especially our teacher/editor, Ariele Huff, whose abilities with the English language are beyond compare. However, all grammatical failings, modern rule avoidance, and typos are my own.

And with extreme thanks to JH, WC, JL, and EP who exemplify the best of the counseling process.

Made in the USA
San Bernardino, CA
06 October 2014